FLOWERS OF SPIT

Catherine Mavrikakis

FLOWERS
OF
SPIT

Translated by
Nathanaël

BookThug 2011

FIRST ENGLISH EDITION
Fleurs de crachat © 2005, Leméac Éditeur (Montréal Canada)
translation copyright © Nathanaël, 2011

The production of this book was made possible through the generous assistance of The Canada Council for The Arts and The Ontario Arts Council.

Canada Council **Conseil des Arts**
for the Arts **du Canada**

ONTARIO ARTS COUNCIL
CONSEIL DES ARTS DE L'ONTARIO

Printed in Canada.

LIBRARY AND ARCHIVES CANADA
CATALOGUING IN PUBLICATION

Mavrikakis, Catherine, 1961-
[Fleurs de crachat. English]
    Flowers of spit / Catherine Mavrikakis ; translated by Nathanaël.

Translation of: Fleurs de crachat.
ISBN 978-1-897388-88-4

    I. Nathanaël, 1970- II. Title. III. Title:
Fleurs de crachat. English.

PS8576.A8579F5313 2011   C843'.6   C2011-904777-2

T.'s spit on me, at the somewhat painful point of orgasm, was the sweetest refreshment, like the spray of a word of love.

– Hervé Guibert, *The Mausoleum of Lovers*

To you, on whom I continue to spit.

One

I RUIN EVERYTHING. That's how it is. Me, Flore Forget, unworthy daughter of my mother, the late Violette Hubert, I have to admit I ruin everything. I screw everything up, make everything go sour. A bad mayonnaise. That's what I make of life. I sack, I ravage, I ruin, I pulverise. I have mad dreams of eradicating ease. Proudly, I swagger, full of myself, looking like a purple soldier with my greedy, smug, G.I. mug. I think desperately of wrenching life from the dung heap on which it grows so abundantly, the whore. I think I'm a gust of wind, a fierce gale, a tidal wave, a north-wester, a tempest. I'm all about the last judgment. I'm pregnant with tactical raids against immensity. I am the justiciary of desperate life.

Like Malborough, Flore goes to war and doesn't know when she'll be back. But she's in every battle, this little mother courage. She guns, she bombs, lays siege and misses her targets. Here she is capsizing, she turns, yes, she turns everything bad. And so it goes, goes, goes, for the little marionettes of misfortune. And so it goes, goes, goes, three little turns and it won't be long... Everything is fucked and for good.

I fight, I combat, I terrorize. I like it when "decent

people" are afraid of me and look upon themselves with distrust. *Let them tremble, let the idiots shudder in my wake,* that's what I say to myself. I scream, I vociferate, I preach in the desert, before the great arrival, the great disembarkment, the violent breaker that will ravage everything. I'll force you all to surrender, bound hand and foot to the victors that are coming, duty bound to come.

I ruin everything, I screw everything up. I've bawled so much, I've bombed decent people to such an extent, riddled them with missiles, that they're even more stunned. They've gone bunker, blockhaus, pillbox, fort, they've made themselves ironclad, shielded themselves with carapaces. And me, I'm a bell sounding the alarm. I'm a bell. Ding, dong! A bell rung wrong, a ring, ring, too sharp, ringing in the ears, a pain in the neck. A limping ding, dring, dring, an electric carillon that's out of synch, that's all askew. Yes, I'm a much too wobbly bell. I can't seem to stop. I find myself stunned, desireless, hopeless. Stop the assault, by God! There's no point pounding over there, there's nobody left. Nothing. Save a giant fracture in the head, a sharp pain reminding me that I used to exist. I'm an armistice, an unremitting truce. I've lost battles, discharged all my bullets and lost everything post-haste. All I have left is my living bodies design job, my medical stylist job, my surgeon job that everyone treats with the respect due to the dead. All I

have now is a mother who left feet first and a poisoned
mind. And frankly, it's best not to have anything at all.

Mother's death was the lowest of the low. The
final offensive, the great bombing. *La ultima vez.* My
last battle. Now it's over. *Auf Wiedersehen* battles and
ultimatums. I capitulate, I surrender. I'm done with
the cause, purity, justice, greatness, with my madness,
with John the Baptist preaching on the battlefied, done
with the Messiah. A dead man doesn't wage war. Things
are going badly, they'll go worse yet. I don't give a shit.
I demand peace and I am certainly not preparing for
any war. I disarm, I denuclearize and demilitarize. I feel
good, my body stuffed full of every imaginable thing,
I'm floating without a parachute, without a giant aircraft
carrier. I'm slowly discovering paradise in my intoxicated
soul. The paradise I prescribe for myself with small doses
of medicine, brand new or very old. Prozac, Marplan.
Ludiomil, Desyrel, Phenelzine, Valium, Elavil, Largactil,
Rivotril, Asendin, Pertofrane, Triadapin, Ativan, Serax,
Zapex, Restoril, Dalmane, Luvox, Zoloft. *Just name it.
The sky is the limit.* And "Lucy is in the sky". My mother
Violette too. My mother… Slowly I'm going to join her
injecting myself full of happiness. Just a little mauve hit.

I'm waving the white flag. I'm making peace
with the whole Earth. I lay myself down at my own
feet and drag my slimy ideas through the muck. I
move on to something else. To nothing especially.

11

To the kaleidoscopic, multicoloured emptiness,
the cosmic emptiness, the emptiness of gellcaps,
capsules, housecoats. *Skinnamarink-a-dinky-dink.*
Skinnamarink-a-doo life hates you. Skinnamarink-a-
dinky-dink. Skinnamarink-a-doo life hates you. It hates
you in the morning and in the afternoon. It hates you in
the evening and underneath the moon. Skinnamarink-
a-dinky-dink. Skinnamarink-a-doo life hates you. I'm a
deserter, a loiterer, I bury the war axe, I smoke the peace
pipe and all the smoke-producing drugs. I don't kill
anything, I don't go to the shooting gallery anymore.
I'm war weary. Now that Mother is dead, there's no
point talking about it. Basta! I feel like an apparatchik
of peace, a pen-pushing peace-maker, a mummy of
harmony. An anesthetist of the living. I stuff myself
full of tranquilisers. Gulp! Gulp! Piles of medications,
drugs, doses of boredom. *Stop agitating yourself, my poor*
Flore, stop. Spit on everyone, but keep a smile on your face,
there, as if nothing had happened. Spit with class, spit into
the wind, and above all not idly, spit fashionably, spit all
the rage, spit hip, spit spun, spit ready-made, gob grand
couturier. I'm going for soft spit, glamour gob. Me, Flore
Forget, I invent invisible spit. Clean spit. The spittle of
bad faith for all. It's my secret missile, my catapulting
thingamajig, my infernal arsenal, my traditional weapon.
I spit on them, but they don't even know it. I purify
myself in the phlegm of my medicated bile and pray to

greedy heaven on my knees that one day my mouth will
dry altogether, deprived of ammunition. I ask, begging,
for the impossible gob in which I will no longer burst…
The spit that will kill without leaving the slightest trace.
End this dirty wa-ar…

Forward march! Like before! We'll rough it like
never before! Now that Mother is decomposing, rotting
in the earth, in the mud, *mud, you'll turn over mud,*
gelatinous mud, sticky mud, viscous mud, muh!, muh!,
I'm learning to close my trap, do like everyone else, the
idiot enemy, fall in line, walk straight. And if I have to
swallow a bunch of pills in psychedelic tubes to do so,
I'll be a good little soldier.

I collaborate, I approve, I compromise, I acquiesce,
I'm all about alliance and renunciation. I'm a giant Yes,
pure consent, I who only ever knew how to say no. It
turned into an illness… It started before me, well before
me. I couldn't have invented this myself. It's in my genes,
as they say. I had a kalachnikov in my blood, a bazooka
in my organs, a submachine gun in my trap. I was of the
Old Guard, a serial killer. A psychopath of waste, but
it's moving through me… Thanks to life, to that bitch
of a life that entered me like a bastard locomotive, like
thundering shrapnel, and thanks, thanks to chemistry.
It's crazy how much I owe you.

My metamorphosis into the vanquished will take
place in five seconds. You can't say it'll drag itself out.

You've got to see it's been preparing itself. It doesn't happen overnight, all this. Never in a single salvo. Metamorphoses and metempsychoses. It works us over, insinuates itself, underhandedly, even if it acts like it doesn't affect us. I was sniped at slowly, strategically. And then one day, like a giant missile, it fell right on top of me! A fulgurating blitzkrieg. An honourless fight. I'm all dizzy from it...

Two months before Mother's death, I saw his head, the Crackpot's head, walking past the windowed opening of the door of my front hall. I saw his mad eyes in ecstasy. Right away I understood that the sacking would have to end. That if I continued so wastefully, I would become like him, with his orgasmically mad mug. I would harrass people, call them up in the middle of the night, show up at their door at five a.m. and stay in their front hall until they came home from their holidays. I was going to go for the state of siege, the bleeding banger. All this to change the world. All this because I speak the truth. But what do I care about being right? What a thought, to be in one's own right? I hadn't seen Florent again, my brother Florent. Hadn't contemplated his crackpot face, high on meds and shock therapies for thirty years now. But when I saw his crazy face in my front hall at eight o'clock in the morning, as I was coming home from the hospital, after a night spent in emergency sewing together pieces of bodies, shreds of bodies, I knew right away that it was him. But that it was also me. I was going to end up like that, in my own front hall at eight o'clock in the morning, waiting for me to come back dead tired from the hospital. I immediately recognised him, the dingo. I said to myself: Hey, it's Florent. After thirty years there's nothing banal about recognising a blissed-out head wandering past the window of my door. It's not everyday I see the madman about to come and think quietly: *There's my brother, the Crackpot, whom I haven't seen for 360 months, 9800 days, give or take.* It was then, exactly then, that I began to understand that something in me was shattered, that I was already potted. Only a nutter could recognise the glimpsed head of Florent, some thirty years hence. This could only ever happen to me. Me, the generalissimo of arrogance, the captain of pride! I, Marshal John the Baptist, who live in a world out of time, a world in which I can always identify the Messiah, denounce the devil, separate the good from the bad, the mad from the sane and more than that, tell my big brother's head apart from that of a simple cretin. After thirty years. That's something worth worrying about.

It was only after having recognised the Crackpot that I realised I was slipping. That there was no reason for me to recognise him, deranged as he was, and instead I should be asking myself what a visibly exalted stranger was doing in my front hall at eight o'clock in the morning. I began to hate that guy. I began to want to rip my brother's head off and maybe rip out his vulgar dilating eyes. I wanted to make mush of that guy whom I could identify with a single look, explode a grenade in his head. It's really a kind of damnation to be able to recognise someone after thirty years. You've got to be pretty cursed to live with all that memory. It's a constant noise in the cranium. The past speaks to me, confabs with me, and even when I was a kid, it was already playing the trick of the thing that comes back. By the age of three, all I had was memory. Memory enough not to know what to do with. Memory to curse the universe for centuries and centuries and voices in my head telling me things, speaking, always speaking, and bespeaking my misfortune. It yells in my brain, it vociferates sense, it mutters something. I'm the victim of a curse, the curse of the noise in the brain. I'm being punished for something. Your guess is as good as mine.

And when I pushed open my front door, the Crackpot fired right at me: *I've been waiting for you for nine hours, I left messages on the machine. A voice whispered to me "Mother's going to die". I decided to come. Where were you? I alerted the United Nations.* But the worst of it is that I – me, me, me – I answered that nutcase as though we had spoken the day before, as though everything were normal, as though there weren't thirty years to fill, thirty years to repair, thirty years to answer for, no? I shot right back at him, at my crazy brother: *I work nights, I do! Moron! My messages? I don't pick them up. You've got no business being in my front hall. And what's more, who told you Mother was sick? What voice?… Who called you? And the United Nations? You've gone off the rails, man! Tomorrow, Mother will have the results from the biopsy of her left breast. But she's not about to die. Are you nuts or what? Where do you come from? It's been thirty years since we've seen you. You think we were still waiting for you? We thought you were dead, disappeared, just killed in action, and we weren't grieving.*

My moronic brother didn't dignify my questions with an answer. He came into my apartment with me. As simple as that. And then, for the two months that followed, for the two months during which Mother agonised with her ravaging cancer, he was constantly under my feet, that half-witted brother of mine, always dragging himself to the hospital with me or squatting in my front hall, always spying on me, keeping me in check.

And he was right, the vile nutcase. I still don't know who told him what, in what omen he recognised mother's death. I still don't know what the voices of heaven or hell whisper to idiots, but that assfucker was right: Mother was going to die. And what's more, it would happen quickly. A really fast cancer, that carries you magnificently away, attacks your whole body, metastasizes before you can blink. Hip! Hip! Those things, they aren't cancers, they're works of art. That's when you think life's an artist. An artist of misfortune, perfected, chiselled, refined. *"Cent fois sur le métier, remettez votre ouvrage polissez-le sans cesse et le repolissez."* That's Boileau. *"A hundred times, consider what you've said; polish, repolish, every colour lay."* Yes, life is a genius of the end. Even when she botches the job, we nonetheless owe her recognition for her talent. All the same, we've got to give a standing ovation to the sublime, to the grand gesture.

At Mother's funeral, all four of us were there in the end, and for us, Genêt and me, it was quite strange to see our mother's whole descendency present. There was the Crackpot, the older son, completely demented and ecstatic, despite the circumstances. There was Genêt, my little brother, the gallerist, freshly arrived from Paris, completely undone, howling in pain, scattering himself in tears. There was me, eyes empty, mouth dry, anesthetised by the meds I'd prescribed myself from the moment at which I had almost profaned Mother's rigid body. I'm the one who found Mother dead. Between two emergencies. And off I go to sew you up another one! And off I go straight away to unstitch myself from life! She left all by herself, like a big girl, while her daughter (me, as it happens), was ligaturing an imbecile whose body was pissing blood, a cretin who had split his

18

head open at top speed on his motorbike, totally drunk.
Those idiots would be better off slowing down! They'd
be better off not drinking like fish, those imbeciles,
those bastards! I wouldn't have to stop up hemmorages
and stitch up miles of human bodies! Lacework isn't my
thing! I'm sick of those schmucks! If there were fewer
of them, I could have been there at the moment of
Mother's death. She wouldn't have gone out alone, like a
dog. She wouldn't have croaked in her sinister room, as
though she'd never brought into the world three potted
children, ingrates, as though she'd never given birth to
a dirty brood of three who let her agonise in the green
solitude of a drab hospital.

Not even like an animal. Because animals,
thankfully, are treated better than that.

Healing bodies, saving souls, recomposing existence.
That's my life. But what good does it do me, I who left
my mother alone to confront death, who wasn't able
to hold her in my arms during her last spasm, my last
battle?

At Mother's funeral, there was also my daughter,
Rose, the little sweetheart, my big Rosie, four years
old, who was playing and laughing and babbling
with the flowers placed near the coffin of her beloved
grandmother.

I hadn't seen the tosspot in public with us, with
Genêt and me, for thirty years. His presence, in that

little church at the east end of the city, five kilometres from where I was used to imagining myself, for better or for worse mind you, made it clear that Mother was very much dead. Her body was cold, rigid and rotting by the second and for eternity among the immortals and the reseda branches. Mother would no longer really be there, not ever there, since, after all, if the nutter had bothered to budge after so many years of silence, it certainly wasn't to see her again... He had come, led by his mad instinct, to sniff out whether there was in Montréal, at Mother's death, some way to repair the breach made in the name of the son. He had come, moved by some mad hope, to sniff the body of his agonising mother in order at last to smell the emanation of a familar and sweet scent that would have assured him that he was her child. The tender, reassuring perfume of maternal flesh, a mad smell of violets, the purple exhalations of life's entrails... But just as the coffin was being closed, even though he'd sniffed the body one last time the way a dog sniffs a bone, nothing had happened. Nothing had gushed out. No more than when they had met, she and he, on the day of the fatal diagnosis, that day on which his head had wandered into my entranceway. No more than on each day that he had visited her during two months of agony, after having systematically harrassed me in emergency. As the coffin was being closed, my brother raised his eyes in ecstasy, the same eyes as in the photographs of him that we kept, when I was a teenager. Once again, he was there for nothing. That son would never have a mother, not even a dead mother. Nothing doing. He had nothing. Except me.

And me, I have to stop the machine of my madness. The little mechanism that makes you loopy. Mother is dead. The Crackpot is fit to be tied. It's all over. I've joined the ranks of the peaceful militias. I'm stopping my games, my warring meanness. I'm returning to the herd of happy imbeciles. I bought some peace. And a Zoloft, if you please! This round is on me.

At the hospital, Mother's agony gives the cowards such joy, those vultures, those dirty little pieces of trash. They finally have something to hold against me, something tangible: *Her mother is dying. She has a psychotic brother who follows her everywhere in the hospital. It runs in the family. We've got her. She's having a breakdown. We'll be able to shut that shit-disturber's trap, that hysterical, pretentious bitch, who always tries to change us, tell us how much better she is than we are. We'll have her hide. As soon as her mother is cold, we'll have her locked up or laid off at least. She'll do something that will allow us to get rid of her. Finally, we'll have some peace. Life, stupid and serene, will just purr right along. We'll be able to pocket our bribes, amass medical errors, speak out of our asses, harrass the nurses, she won't be here anymore to denounce us. Clear the floor, bitch! Her mother can't die soon enough.*

Enough! Let her kick it as well!

A breakdown? Yes, that may explain the desire not to yell anymore, not to shriek with pain at the force of people's inertia. I'm familiar with the remedies, even if I'm not a psychiatrist, even if I'm just a Dr. Frankenstein who patches up corpses in the making.

Since the Crackpot's arrival and the beginning of the process of Mother's decomposition at the cemetery, I've lost my taste for blood. There are no more hostilities. The psychiatrists are right, I'm having a breakdown. A real one. A big one. A blatant, normalising breakdown. Not a permanent depression, the one that is my revolution. No, a breakdown like anyone else, a dulling of all the senses and intelligence, which will allow me to function at the drop of a hat, but not too quickly, but at a pace in complete synchronicity with their lethargy.

I was still considering putting up resistance when I saw the Crackpot harrass me in Emergency, while Mother was agonising on the ninth floor of the hospital. I began to think furiously as Mother's cancer was swallowing her body, devouring our minuscule joy in life. How stupid we become when we set about meditating... I thought of that terrible life which always wins and which dropped us on Earth. I wasn't ready to feel nothing, I wasn't quite prepared to call up my mediocrity with all my strength, to consider death a necessity, find a reason, tell myself loudly and clearly:

Mother is old, Mother lived. Death is natural. It's not a scandal... I was still resisting the dreadful, the depravity. I was the front line against the horror of life. But now, it's good and done. I've suffered too much. I demand to be anesthetised, chemically tethered.

Only once I'd found Mother's cold body did I really realize the gravity of my problem! I'd taken on dangerous, troubling, monstrous proportions. I was simply too human. I wanted to do everything, understand everything, howl, suffer, think and everything else, everything else. It was scoffing my brain.

It's true, I'm having a breakdown. And since I'm a doctor, a fixer of all sorts, and it's my responsibility to bring aid to people in danger, I prescribe myself the best of the best. The champagne of antidepressants, in addition to several vintage wines: anxiolitics. They age well, keep well at room temperature, are long in the mouth. I'm giving myself a little treat. Some anxios. Just for the taste. And then I strongly recommend a spot of analysis to myself. It's probably not very useful, but it can't hurt. I'll go and lay myself out on the couch, contemplate a dull ceiling and speak of my accursed childhood, of Florent's fissures, of Mother's death, of my daughter, my beloved lineage. I'll go invent a story for myself, my own story. Or that of a girl who could have been me, if I'd had something resembling a life.

Mother is dead. I swallow everything. I know my

classics. I'm a doctor, aren't I? I'll soon move over
to the monoamine oxidase inhibitors (MAOI) or
nonselective monoamine reuptake inhibitors, including
imipramine, which have always been a temptation… I'll
try everything, everything that's available on the health
market… I've got to get to work, get on the relentless
task of normality. I've really been lazy on that front…
How slothful I've been! Mother has been dead for two
weeks. She was buried eleven days ago. But I have always
been miserable, since the dawn of time, the night of
childhood. And it doesn't get any better on the full
moon. The Crackpot is somewhere in my apartment,
squatting in my life. I don't care. I'm sick of my chronic
migraines, the facial pain that blows my head apart.
And then I grind my teeth, night and day. The sound
of these jaws accompanying my days is wearisome. The
grrr, grrr that competes with the din of my brain is
exhausting. Mother has passed on, but I hold happiness
in a coloured vial set upon a red couch. I lure ecstasy
with my prescriptions. And I'll sign another one for
myself. It's the good Flore Forget who is prescribing
this again for me. Thank you, doctor! I'll lie down in
bliss, a disciple of Freud behind me, just behind the
couch. I'll bring the house down once and for all with
a Molotov cocktail of antidepressants and let myself be
swallowed by the void of a quiet life, a sweet life, the life
of everyone. I'll abandon the Crackpot's misfortune and

leave squalor to the nutters. I hand over my lightning tomahawks, my weapons of destruction. I'll no longer think of Mother's face as I'm falling asleep. I won't see her eaten by death, raped by worms, filled a little more each day, with the earth around her, invading her.

Happy, happy. Therefore will I be happy. For me, it's nothing other than the happiness of this monumental collective depression, this general cease-fire, good and wily, good and bright. Hip! Hip! I'll sign all the treaties, conclude all the pacts. I'm stopping my tank here, ceasing the artillery fire. Into the regiment of life, I will recruit myself. I do intend to enlist in the squadron of mutilees of hope, of roaming cripples. Wait up. I'm coming...

Two

THE PROBLEM, YOU see, is that I've thought it
through, too much, you might say, it's typical of you: to
tell me not to think, to let me go off, lose my grip
especially, say everything that's going through my mind,
but in this case, you're so completely mistaken and I
don't know why I'm bringing the king into it now, I
mean the queen, the Queen of England, maybe the
Queen of England who was wrong to have thought ill of
Lady Diana... you know I'm the same age as Lady
Diana, I mean the same age she would have been, she's
dead, and me, I'm alive and it always surprises me, that I
outlive myself, not to have croaked when I was young,
not to have kicked the bucket out of fear, or not to have
dangled myself from a rope, but... hey, you, pen-pusher,
you're writing it down... what are you writing, mister
shrink? certainly not a life's work... that I'm suicidal
maybe? because you might otherwise forget, hey? you
might mistake me for another woman who's always
happy, in a good mood, who comes here simply to solve
the problems of her tender breasts or her chronic
constipation, and which you, you have diagnosed as
psychosomatic? and yet one needn't have much of a
memory to recall that I'm a good candidate for flinging

myself onto the other side of life in five seconds flat, all you have to do is look at my crazy face, the face of a depressed, medicated person, to imagine me with very little effort at the end of a rope, or even better to think of my corpse, a projectile launched directly onto the pavement from the hospital roof, my soft corpse, like a big pile of meat, an ugly packet of shit, I'd go *plop!* at the bottom, just a big plop! come on, I know what people who throw themselves from buildings look like, people who throw themselves head first into death and into the plop! of themselves... do you think people hear themselves go plop! or that they're too dazed by the fall and the pain? because you know, you shouldn't underestimate pain, a real horror, it shrieks, the body speaks, even conked out, there are bodies that go on braying hours after death, in the violence of dying, of being torn from this shit life... bodies cry out, without a doubt, they shriek at death, and I've had my share in emergency, of people crushed by their lives, you can't say as much, suffering, for you, is nothing but a bunch of boneheads like me who confide in you on this crimson couch they sink into so comfortably, it's true these are nice cushions, they could make you forget everything, but that's exactly it, here, there's still a little push of memory, nothing can be overlooked, everything must be said slumped on these cushions that favour sleep... I'd like some just like these, but I think it would remind me

too much of something like here, something like these
bad memories, not those of my past, those of a
psychoanalyzed, dismembered present, where I find
myself sprawled across a bloody couch... objects are
powerful, after all, they have an impact... suffering,
violence, are abstractions, words... none of your patients
shit on you, scratch you, slap you, you know it's
happened to me several times, several small times, I don't
keep track... you've never been punched in the face, and
it's likely no one defecated on your beautiful, red
cushions, so crimson, so rousing of my violence... I'll
initiate you one day if you want, it's a promise, it will
give us some relief, you and me... you dream of going
hand to hand with your patient, you feel a bit lonely in
your armchair where no one, but no one, touches you...
it gives you the sense that you're already dead for never
having been looked at by your patients, doesn't it? it's
awful, all this indifference, yours, yes, yours... and then,
of course, there is mine... I'm not here to spare myself,
to bolster myself, I know what I'm worth, not much, I
know... psychoanalysts remind me of stiff cadavers, they
are absolutely not supple, always stiffening before the
signifier, the signifier, it makes you hard doesn't it? you're
writing that down, I hope... it's not because someone
touches you that you get all hard, it's because words have
an effect on you... it's a little Priapic side, for sure, you
have that, you have a boner all day long since the

signifier always comes on time, even when it plays hide-and-seek, it comes, at a given moment, at a turn of phrase... yes, there it is, the good signifier, and then, really, you can't take it anymore, and you get hard again for another little hour... you inscribe the signifier in your big yellow notepad, so that you can have another boner in the evening on your own or with your colleagues on the phone or in seminars, you never unload, that would be too much, it's crazy what words, it's powerful, in fact, but objects too, and bodies, bodies, they're so... fragile... a body shattered by a fall, a body shrieking in pain, you don't know what that is, you'd have to look without getting hard and I'm not sure you're capable of that, it's true chose you for that very reason, because I heard you get good and hard, that the signifier puts you in such a state, so much the better, you are, apparently, an excellent psychoanalyst, and I am an excellent patient, so everyone says, says I should go see a shrink, because I've got everything it takes, well here I am, I hope you're good and hard... that body, an almost beloved body, splattered on the sidewalk after a ten-storey fall, I swear it wasn't pretty, it was awful... I don't want to tell you... mind you, I was never in a war hospital, surely there's worse, but it's nonetheless traumatizing, don't think the length of the fall always determines the state of the body, no, I've seen twenty-storey falls that are still fairly recognizable and then a guy who threw himself from the

fourth floor in a really disturbing state... I have my
theories about that: the stiffness of the body as it falls
doesn't help things, you've got to let yourself go, be
loose, what I was saying earlier, at the beginning of the
session, if you remember a single thing I've said, if you're
taking notes as you should in your notebook or in your
mess of a memory... one musn't harden while falling, just
try to glide like an airplane, mind you, gravity still has
the upper hand, I know, I'm not an idiot, I see the
results, but it's good to believe for a moment that one is
flying away... you've absolutely got to believe it, at least
for a second, to have the courage to push off, the
courage to give yourself up, give it all up... if one believes
in flight even a little bit, I'm sincerely convinced that the
fall is less harsh, mind you, this is just conjecture, the
obscure and morbid ravings of a surgeon who's learning
on the fly, on the flying leap of cadavers with her
medical knowledge, I haven't done a study, I'm not
talking statistics, this is all from experience... do you
understand the degree to which my profession is a
traumatism? that it's out of defiance that I open and
close those bodies?... O.K., so I chose this rotten job,
but I was already traumatized, already exhausted,
permeated with life and its matter... throughout my
childhood my dreams were strewn with pieces of
bodies... arms, hands, brains, organs, scattered, in
heaps...I closed my eyes to find myself once again with

decomposing bodies or scraps of flesh, it's still that way,
when I'm not careful enough, when I don't stuff myself
full of medication or when I don't collapse in a heap of
exhaustion, after thirty-six hours on call and who knows
how many surgeries, I start to dream of cut up limbs
again, like when I was small... and when Mother died, it
almost caught up with me again... I always wanted to be
a surgeon, it was a true vocation, a passion, I drove
everybody crazy with medicine, at the age of three,
already, I knew this about myself and when I was asked
what I wanted to do later, I could answer without
hesitation, at the age of three, with honesty, it's not
everyday and it pissed people off, such will, such
assurance, such determination... only my mother knew
it was real and that nothing, but nothing could stop me,
my mother always talked to me about World War Two,
Normandy, the rotten bodies encountered during the
exoduses, the extraction of her older sister, Madame
Muchembled's, kidney and brains on the road, and that
her own husband had to put back into the cranial cavity
after having wiped away the shrapnel... Madame
Muchembled had held on to some remnants of her brain
in the gutter, apparently she loses her memory from time
to time, intermittently, like all of us, to get through this
fucking life, you don't have to be Funes in Borges's text...
you read? better off having Alzheimer's in the
forgottenness of all words, no? after that scene, my

mother never ate offal again, never; there's also the story
of that woman in the green coat who was decapitated by
a bomb right next to my mother, in a trench, she, my
mother, told me the whole story, when I was a child...
the coat was still good, after the decapitation, still green,
the colour of hope, so they say... she's eaten her share of
mad cow, my mother has, but never, I repeat, offal, me I
eat nothing but that: kidney, brains, liver, and I know
what I'm eating, I'm a surgeon, I can say that I know
what I'm talking about... even as a small child, I wanted
to sew up all the bodies that worked me over in the
night, I wanted to piece together history, stitch white
thread into everything, but as soon as I began my
medical training, I understood that more than anything
I would be a butcher cutting up my share of brisquet in
order to be good and fat when I kick it, to parody Boris
Vian, would you like me to sing? before learning to sew,
even before learning a single thing... one day, something
clicked inside my head, I had chosen this profession
because in the end, I had wanted to learn how to make
sausage meat, I'm like the Head of State who goes first, I
like blood and brawn, there's no greatness in my calling
to the needle point, there's just my desire to colour in
red, to unstitch from the life that's left a bit of gristle for
me to bite into, savagely, like a beast, a bit of flesh and I
want it, with all the aggression in me, I could let go of
just like that, from one day to the next... at least that's

what I tell myself... I've always dreamed of bodies that make no sense, shredded, dismembered, decapitated bodies, heads that roll on their own, without gathering moss, that's all my dreams are made of, wherever I walk, I step in a piece of flesh, I can't bloody walk on solid ground it's worse than walking on eggshells, worse than a march or die and worse even than marching into combat, worse than anything, I walk on humain remains, sometimes they're still warm, and at every turn I run the risk of falling, of rolling around in the mire of organisms, I stumble into carrion, I make much of viscous remains, I roll around in the hospital dumpsters, that's what my nights are made of, I mean, before I started taking my meds, the little pills that glaze me, my very own pill... I don't know why I keep speaking in the present, because now, I see everything in colour, just colours, I'm given to such psychedelia, I don't dream anymore, I paint, Picasso didn't invent anything, he must have been taking psychotropics... you see, the present, speaking in the present, it's that somehow it doesn't let go, it doesn't loosen its grip... oh! the signifier... I can feel you harden, yes? it's all I can do to stuff myself full of gellcaps, this and that, I know I'm stuffed full of all that suff, that the only solution would be to fly off a Montréal peak, off one of the roofs of the world and not miss my flight 61 to the beyond, I think it would be the only way to stop seeing all that semi-

putrefied or squirming flesh, the only way to stop the
machine of death, I'd thumb my nose at it, grab the bull
by the horns, yeah, I'd go faster than it does, I die before
it finishes me, that would be clever... I'm going to tell
you something, mister shrink, you'll note that I don't
call you "doctor", because here, I'm the doctor, and
frankly, doctors are people I don't trust, I mean really...
Dr. Forget, she's so sick of everything she'd blow up the
hospital if she weren't afraid of being the on-call surgeon
that day, if she weren't quaking before the eventuality of
having to sew up all her colleagues, whom she'd be quite
happy to bleed like cattle, but she has ethics, that idiotic
Dr. Forget... death would cure me of the decomposition
of the entire world, I'd be done with this carcass of a
life... there's only death to deliver me from death, I don't
know what I'm waiting for and why I waited so long, in
fact, why didn't I do myself in like Lady Di as in "you
die" or "live and let die", I thought you'd like that... for
me to let myself go, I mean, in English especially
because I don't speak English badly at all, it's part of my
success, yes, it's true, one must speak English when one
is a surgeon, when one has studied at McGill, it's got to
pay off somehow... I didn't just learn the profession of
butcher, of renderer of human livestock, morcellater of
meat and scalper of cadavers, I didn't only learn how to
handle the knife, the scalpel and the big scissors, I
degreased my mind, I learned English to be able to

converse with the big shots of the profession and have it off with the scientific reviews that are advancing medical research... my daughter's father was a Canadian who bored me to tears, a guy from somewhere else, the Prairies, a guy who was always between two states, two countries, two girlfriends, two chairs, two cars and two operations... an Anglophone surgeon, he had everything going for him, everything to please me, so it seemed... Rose doesn't look like him, at least I don't think so, not yet... she looks more like a woman I lived with for several years, a woman I loved very much but left because I was throwing myself from the hospital roof from time to time, I was drawn to the void and I was ruining everything, always everything, I was given to suicide repeatedly, thinking myself pure, ever uncompromising... well, that was all a long time ago, I mean, after the pills, before Mother's death, because now, it's over... the wasted life is over. I haven't said so yet but I fall in love with men and with women, without distinction, yes, yes... I don't make a distinction, I who live in the bodies of others, well, in sexuality and love, I mix everything up, I grab at everything, I catch as catch can, oh now there's an expression: catch as catch can, I never say: fountain, I'll never drink of your water... I know, I know you appreciate these metaphors, it's crazy how excited you shrinks can get over such things, so I'm giving you your money's worth, I'm not stingy... how much is this damn session costing me, a hundred and twenty-five dollars for forty-five minutes? it's really not a bad price, I'm a surgeon, I've got money, I'd have more if my stitchings were more aesthetic, but you really can't say I'm not earning a good living, I must be as rich as you are, maybe even more... hey, you didn't expect me to be so mean, but alas, yes, in the end, I'm sure I'm much better paid than you are, in three quarters of an hour, I earn much more, I'm not telling you how much, I don't want to hinder your counter-transference, go on, fantasise, fantasise about my poverty, about my psychoanalytic ruin, I sense you're less hard now... fantasy isn't really your thing... you don't really know the imaginary, there's only the symbolic for you... the problem, my dear, is that though money may be symbolic, it is also real, and thus must I tell you that in the real, I earn much more than you do, it's a misfortune, but I had to be paid more, because a hundred and twenty-five dollars is nothing, peanuts... I'm not even getting off on what I just paid you, I've got to believe I'm not paying a high enough price... in all of this, I must tell you that I take almost no pleasure... for me, orgasm is a kind of consumption, yes... one, two, three... usually, I've wrapped it up... and I've sealed it for you in no time... I go, I'm gone, I go again, I come again, I bubble and burst, I fry my little onions, I fry everything, including the fusebox... and off it goes again... I come every time, I'm a coming machine, an executioner of pleasure, a Swiss watch... it's all in the precision, like a serial killer... I'm the one who puts myself to death, who delivers the death blow, fast, fast... next time will be even better... a steep climb, a rise, a real ascent by paroxystic strikes... to the seventh sky, all the way to the end... the discharge comes, fast and furious, because it's always too much... I can't contain myself... I eat salvo, I devour my libido, I engulf urges, I swallow pleasure... shakes, starts, stops, sackings, give me more... yes, I'll one-up you, reoffend, get my fill, ejaculate, relieve myself and come again... it's a savagery to come like that *ad nauseam, ad lib, adlibitum, ad hominem, ad vitam aeternam* and what's more... and more... that's what I tell myself when I consider the questions... it's a fever, a high high fever, quakes, convulsions, epilepsies... I've got to discharge my revolver of words into the first come ear, then all the jism my body's capable of... like a man, I know, worse than a man, because what's more... and more... it's a question of economy, and overbidding and expenditure... I can operate on my patients on an assembly line, like I can come one more time, repetition brings me back to life, even exhausted, I find pleasure in things again... it's all I know, the reprise, once again, one more time, the same thing, please... more, a hundred times, a thousand times, a hundred thousand times, let it start over, endlessly, more, more, more, don't stop... at

last, it's over, woah! because even with the meds I'm
taking, forget about such craziness, the pills put Dr.
Forget in neutral, on ice, at rest, at a standstill... I'm
done for, finished... really, I should just give up surgery,
I'm every bit an anaesthetist now... put the senses to
sleep, paralyse the world, shush whatever makes noise,
appease things, beings, erase the horror, resorb it into a
semi-coma, in the cottony whiteness of my mind, that's
my new vocation, make it be quiet, stop moving, while
waiting for the ablation, the definitive ablation of all
sensitivity, but I'm not there yet, I still haven't broken
with everything... I've got to learn, to neutralise myself
further, to defuse myself... more medication, I beg of
you, right now, otherwise, I swear it, I won't make it, I
won't be able to put up with all this shit, I mean
Mother's death, Florent's return, and the four years of
my Rose, I won't... I can't... I was sixteen the first time...
I told myself: it can't start, I can't take this... I can't... a
trip to Chicago, a visit to my godmother Marie, like me,
Flore Marie Forget... a little visit to see my godmother,
Marie Brower, and her husband, an old American
soldier... during World War II... my first driver's
license... a trip to Chicago... in the car, on the way, I was
already a sight for sore eyes... paranoia on the American
road... a Sartrian nausea was making me crazy... visions
of my body eviscerated in a Michigan rest area, images
of the four of us disembowelled after eating our

sandwiches, I was hallucinating the distribution of
family pieces in the dumpsters along midwestern
highgways... it really is clean, in the United States, all
things considered... but I was convulsive in the motels at
night... there was me, Mother, Florent and Genêt... all
of us... the Fenouillard family on an expedition... it was
the last time we would all be together... the last... three
months later, Florent became the Crackpot, Genêt left
for Paris to study Fine Arts in solitude and Mother
remarried a whole new husband... I was losing her... I
was going to live alone... I can't remember where...
somewhere near the parc Lafontaine, I think, since in
the evenings, I made a bunch of friends walking my dog,
they slept and fucked where my dog pissed... that trip
was the end... the end of the Forget cell... after that,
everything was lost... I forgot childhood, I forgot my
Mother, I mean my little Mother of love that I covered
in kisses in the evening, and Florent, of course, Florent,
whom I didn't blame, couldn't think about for over
thirty years... Genêt opened a gallery, made a life for
himself in France, we see him twice a year, he calls, we
stay in touch... that's what Chicago was... the city in
which I was born, I don't know if I told you that, the
city in which the family sort of became extinguished...
the last time together... I must have sensed something,
surely I saw it coming, because really, I was so anguished
in Chicago... and on the road... it was physical...

40

terrorized by life, I didn't want to move at all anymore...
play dead... not let myself be taken by the world, the
world with its big mouth full of teeth, ready to tear me
to shreds... Chicago, at night, at Marie's, that was really
the first time... I mean there, the truth appeared to me
in a way... at night, at Marie's, in my little room, with
the sound of trains all night, the sound of trains
whistling in the night, screeching, high-tailing it out of
there, howling to death... I could see myself on the way
to the concentration camps... I could see myself as a Jew
and soon reduced to ash, to dust, cries and then
nothing... shrillness and silence... for all eternity... silence
for the rest of History... and then, five minutes later,
always another train... I didn't really know what trains
were... I'd seen them in films... I was raised in America
in the city, in a motorized suburb... I'm not familiar with
trains... wagons, convoys, are Europe, World War II, and
my mother who fled under American, British and
Canadian shellfire... sirens are D-Day, chaos, bombed
populations, the French and the Germans have got to
retreat... we strike everything in our way on the road to
freedom... trains, that's where you go because you don't
want to go, cattle cars, the locomotive, and at the end,
extermination... Chicago, that night, it was Germany,
1942, Normandy, 1944, it was the war, terror, and then
silence... we cry out and then we don't talk about it
anymore... but it always comes back to haunt us... war,

CATHERINE MAVRIKAKIS

atrocity... that image of a mother shrieking because her
child is being torn from her... in books, on the
television, we learn that these were the most difficult
mothers, the most hysterical, the ones who didn't respect
orders, the good order of the camp... they shrieked, they
hit, they revolted, the mothers of little children... we'll
exterminate you, OK, we kill your children, we reduce
them to nothing, okay... but we don't separate you from
your young, we cannot separate you from your
children... the thought of not seeing them die is
unbearable... we don't accept silence in the place of cries
at the moment of death... their cries of desperation
before the extraction... little ones should die in our
arms... it's a horrific image to behold of that mother who
goes to her death without her daughter or her son,
young, young, a mother who dies thinking her child will
see death alone, abandoned, terrorised, in the ablation of
the mother, in the amputation of the child... silence,
we're cutting... an axe really is necessary to separate a
child from its mother... you really need to slash the
bodies to execute such a rupture, such dismemberment...
all of this haunted me in Chicago, in 1972... full stop
that's all and I didn't sleep that night, the night of my
arrival at Marie's, my godmother, and not any of the
other nights either... I was losing it... me, the little Jew,
little Anne Frank who would die disembowelled by the
American troops, in the chaos of D-Day... I was

42

distrustful of everyone... I wasn't eating anymore, I was
trembling, raving, I was sweating day and night, I didn't
want to confide in anyone... and yet I did say a few
words to Florent... I had spoken to him of the affair and
of the plot against me, against us, the past war and the
war to come... I often thought that bastard stole my
sickness, that he sucked up my psychosis, in Chicago...
Gulp, gulp... I told everything to that nutcase, and he
took off, the screwball, some three months later, and we
didn't hear anything more from him... from time to
time, a well written letter, in fine, tight handwriting, on
letterhead, written by the head of some psychiatric
establishment in France, Germany or Italy, in which
Florent was seeking refuge after having vociferated in the
streets and threatened the worst to passers-by... asylums,
that's where the Crackpot sought shelter... from time to
time we received several words about him... not much,
in the beginning, especially in the beginning, yes, and
then nothing... emptiness, silence... years without a
word, without a sign... just a blank... from him, nothing,
nothing for thirty years, except for that letter, once, at
the beginning also, I mean shortly after his having left, a
letter in which he spoke to us of the bell... a bell in a
child's book, the bell that had called him, that had rung
him, summoned him to leave... a bell that had always
rung wrong, a bell that was askew, as it were... a real bell,
that brother, a cracked bell, indeed... my trains made

him hear the bell of childhood... that guy has an
orchestra in his head... a brouhaha of thunder, it
detonates, carillons... I'd spoken to him of my trains, the
whistling in the night, and there he goes and starts to
hear bells ringing, it wouldn't stop... before splitting, he
would strike up: "Frère Jacques, morning bells are
ringing" at all hours of the day... we were wrung,
wrung... I'm making you laugh, eh? the signifier doesn't
let up... but seriously, I insist on believing that that guy
stole my psychosis... I even think he came back to return
my goods to me, to give unto Caesar what is Caesar's...
because it's crazy how unhinged I've become since his
return... bells that return from Rome and Europe at
Easter can only make a person mad... Mother died on a
Good Friday... I don't know if I mentioned that...
anyway, surely you'd forgotten?... after the train episode
and my life as Anne Frank, we quickly returned to
Montréal, fast, fast, I was rapidly repatriated, I spent
several weeks at my father's in Québec City, he had a
friend who was a pedopsychiatrist... a true friend who
could prescribe something for sleep... an anesthetist, you
know, like me, now... things returned to order... I have
no idea how the anguish was resorbed for a time, no
idea... because it always comes back, when I'm not
paying attention... something ended up saving me from
the trains, I missed them, the trains of 1972, I stayed on
the platform... it may have been a combination of

circumstances that allowed me to pull through, at least
for a time... was it sleep, the air of Montréal, my father,
was it the distance from Chicago, from Europe, a
distancing... why Europe in Chicago? I don't know,
often I thought my illness was the Second World War...
the malady of the last century, the malady of my mother,
of one of Europe's daughters, a daughter of the war... I
always thought I looked like a German... I've never
managed to liquidate history... and yet, it wasn't mine...
not even my own... with my father, I had a sense of well-
being... my father was a strapping lad, a Québécois
through and through, a dentist, an extractor of teeth, a
man who removed boo boos... *come here I'll pull out your
pain,* and he was able... for a time... his wife Céline just
as sturdy as him... an orthodontist who set life right and
straightened teeth *illico presto*... they were good to me
when I got back from Chicago... insanely good... Céline
stuck braces to my teeth and presto... a real pro... my
gums were barded with wire... the three fathers are like
that, tough guys... Mother chose similar men, almost
brothers... it comes back with each lover, with each
pregnancy... three children, three vigorous fathers, three
robust Québécois... but it was my mother who was our
centre of gravity... a small family... a family of crazies...
but we don't have Mother's name... me, I'm a Forget...
she didn't want to pass on her name, her own name:
Hubert... my mother's name was Violette Hubert, a

pretty name, but not what she wanted for us... my mother wanted to forget... the past, her family, her name... I don't know my uncles well, I barely know my aunts... never met my grandfather... after the war, only my grandmother was left... I don't know much about them... my mother had forgotten everything... except that, those pieces of bodies, D-Day, several railway sounds, hunger too, hunger, in the end, I mean... and the war, she gave it to me, she contaminated me with it... I am World War II... I am a battlefield in Normandy... I am an extermination camp in Germany or Poland... I'm the hunger that grips the stomach... I am the uncooked potatoes that are eaten, starving in the fields, I am that... I am fear in the stomach... the sound of boots; the fear at the sound of shoes on the tile... and the defecations upon seeing one's death in a trench... I am that, yes, the defecations, because that's what my nights are, do you hear me? you don't know what my nights are made of... putrefying bodies, mass graves and human excrement... I ought to be exorcised... all those bodies in pieces, cut up, burnt to ashes, dismembered, dead, dead, dead, do you hear death?... the sound of trains, the sound of tanks, the sound of my mother Violette Hubert's name, it's all of that... and that's what my days are, corpses, sick people, limbs I glue back on, things I put end to end, and then the death I anesthetise by anesthetising myself, the death I want to kill with scalpel blows, *well, you, little cunt, you can be sure I'll get you...* I'm a surgeon... not a war surgeon, but in a hospital... on every front, I fight for justice, for truth and also against the filth of death... but what is it to live, if it means dying on an operating table or in a bombing?... what the hell are we doing?... forever asking the same questions, about life, about this rotten death?... enough already... all my life, I've wanted to reveal the scandal, denounce the evil, the idiocy, the absurdity of humans who continue to behave as though all is well, I'd wanted to be the Knight of the Apocalypse... either let's be done with it or let's do something right, something great... but I spoiled everything, without realising it... I was ruining my life... and then the Crackpot showed up, Mother is dead, I went off the rails, came off the rim, my sights dimmed, I heard the sound of trains, and it started up again just like in '14, '42, in '44 and especially in '72, in 1972, Chicago... I was sixteen... it's a good thing I have my meds, really I can only thank science... and Freud a little bit, just the same, a tiny little bit... and you, you, from time to time, you who do help me a bit nonetheless, with what I'm not sure, but still, I sense that you are doing me good, an impression, you make an impression, there... a certain impression, not just anesthetising, not just sedative, you are my artificial paradise... another thing, yes, another thing... I'm attached, I'm attached to you, to these sessions... I often think that Florent should come see you, that he should be the one delivering himself on your couch and rolling around on your crimson cushions... it's like I'm living someone else's madness, even if I have the firm conviction at the same time that he pilferred my psychosis... I had the copyright on my psychosis didn't I?... OK, it wasn't entirely mine, all of it, maybe a fair bit belonged to my mother and then to her father, amputated from the Great War, his right leg amputated... members, pieces of the past wandering around, transmitting themselves from generation to generation, from parent to child, from brother to sister... nothing ever complete, integral, finished, but instead always, always morcellated, cut up, dismembered, dead bits... there is the night, there is death... and especially since her death... I loved my mother so much, I don't remember ever having had the slightest serious argument with her, I loved her so much... the rigid cadaver of my mother, cold in the middle of the room, a giant white room... my mother livid, bloodless, white, yes, in her nightgown, her mortific fabric, stretched out at the centre of that room, all white, like her... something like alabaster, a very pure marmoreal death, majestic, dignificed, very dignified... the peace I hadn't known her to have had when I found her cold and curled up on her hospital bed... my mother died alone while I was operating on a patient who'd opened his thorax in a car,

or something along those lines, I forget... my mother
died all alone... I don't think I'll ever forgive myself, I
don't think that's something one forgives... it would be
too easy... there's no peace in life, or in death... and yet
I'm trying really hard... my dream is whispering
something to me... I'm recounting last night's dream to
you, last night's dream of cadavers, my last dream, my
dream, still warm, of a cold body, all peaceful, and then
it changes, it gets ruined, everything decomposes... a dog
arrives to eat her, my mother, an all black dog, very
scary, with yellow eyes, long, messy, dirty, tousled fur, a
mean dog, very ugly, a hyena, a carrion-feeder, but it's
also a crow, a nasty bird of misfortune, like the
Crackpot, the one who came to announce Mother's
death to us... damn crow... damn dream... that
loathsome beast sniffs my mother, circles her, lunges at
her, biting her... it never stays on Mother's white body
for very long, but as soon as it approaches, it quickly
tears off bits of flesh, bits of white, which expose the
black, rotten meat full of worms... the bird-dog eats my
mother and exposes the body's vermin, the body become
swollen, gnawed by thick worms, and me, me, I'm there,
powerless, I watch the scene without being able to act, I
can't do a thing, but I see, I observe, I have a violent
desire to kill that animal, with my scalpel, my surgical
pliers... I want to dismember that nasty mutt... it
torments me, crucifies me, but there's nothing I can do,

I can't... that's the way it is, the way it's always been... I
reason with myself... there's nothing I can do. I made the
Hippocratic oath... I won't use all that to commit a
murder... the dog squeals... it lets out loathsome,
smothered sounds, strident yelping that raises the hair
on my back... craw, craw, craw, I want to ring the
chimera's neck, reduce the old crow to nothing, rip off
the head, the eyes, the beak and the rest... alouette... gentille
alouette, alouette, je te plumerai, et les yeux, et le bec et la
tête, ah... but I am simply paralysed, I haven't a shred of
strength left... the crow stops, silence, he's satisfied, the
monster won't eat until the end, the vile creature... it's
up to me to finish the job, to masticate my mother, to
digest her, I start taking pieces of the corpse and
chewing them, and then I attack the worms, I devour... I
devour the refuse... I don't know how all this is possible,
to eat one's dead mother... and all those worms, really,
but I do it, my hunger is brutal, a great hunger for flesh
and blood... in my dream, I remember thinking of
Oedipus, of certain unavoidable loves, and then of
Bataille, a text of Bataille's on his taste for the dead, his
love for his mother, his incestuous necrophilia, but I've
never read anything on how to eat one's dead mother,
how to finish off the decaying cadaver of one's own
Mother, I wake with a start... you're the only one who
knows the recipe, the recipe of the mother *au corbeau,* of
the raw mother *au* satisfied crow... unsalted, really

unsalted and without a single condiment... just a dead
mother, several white worms and a giant good and
loathsome canine crow... you cook it all together not too
long... as long as childhood, say... as long as a life or
two... don't let it simmer too much, it's the sort of thing
one eats rare... one of my colleagues at the hospital, a
surgeon like me, but she's an ophthalmologist, was
telling me one day that her French mother had eaten
some dead crow during the war... she'd found a bird on
the road and had started to salivate right away... a dead
crow, she'd loved it... you'd think, it's still meat, flesh...
in the middle of the war, a luxury... her mother was
pregnant... pregnant with her daughter Françoise, the
eye surgeon... her mother licks her chops over a dead
crow: you know, when you're pregnant you have
cravings... there are more than just pickles with whipped
cream, and then it was the war... Françoise ate high
crow, despite herself, foetal ingestion... she consumed
dead bird... I don't remember the context in which she
told me this... she was laughing with me ... my dream is
the just return of things, it isn't the daughter who eats
the crow, but the mother who is devoured... I loved my
mother so much... I understand cannibals, you know... I
loved everything about her, even her Maccabean air at
the hospital, even her very fragile body... and I let her
die alone, and I let her die... I'm no oncologist... what
could I do? I'm just a surgeon... when I lose a patient, it's

awful... I only recover from it very slowly... it's awful not to kill death, not to vanquish it, to bawl it out to the end... *You're going to do as you're told, dirty bitch, lie down at my feet, I'm in charge here...* I'm a doctor and I'm fighting against you... this dream, I don't know... I don't know anything more... I don't see much of anything in all of this... there's only you, mister therapist, to help me digest life... assimilate my mother's body, the war bodies, ugly bodies and crows, in the maternal transit, you know... today I'm all dyspepsia, bloating and flatulence... it stays stuck in my throat, it's on my chest... I want to vomit my whole life onto the couch, regurgitate my mother for you... I woke up this morning feeling like there were thousands of wriggling white worms in my mouth... I woke, my mouth full of my mother... I had a terrible urge to spew, and then it passed, I took my meds, I went through my day calmly, surely, without trouble, thanks to chemistry and its marvellous little multicoloured pills, then I went to the hospital, several well-calculated jabs with my scalpel, and here I am, on your crimson cushions, here I am... and then, tonight, it will be the hospital again, I'm on duty, a regular day, all told... the meds aren't perfect... I still blame it for not always sparing me the worse... the nightmares and everything else... One therapist promised me I'd never dream again, as if... I need to go see that idiot, must stop the machine of corpses, stop the images in my head... I

want to have my brain frozen... I want it to stop its
production in the night... this dream mechanism works
on its own, this dream mechanism... it's inhumane to let
people suffer like beasts nowadays... there must be more
effective substances, I can't believe... honestly...
sometimes I tell myself there's only you... I tell you my
life and the lives of others, my mouth filled with the
pieces of the past... I come to you to swallow all of that,
to drink the cup down to the last drop and put my
entrails to work... I come here to intestinate myself,
ingest everything, digest everything... I eat pieces in my
dreams, all the bits of corpses and flesh lying around,
and I come to you to digest them... you are my
gastroenterologist... you watch the entries and exits...
you take care of the shit, the shit of life... you follow,
direct all that rot through my organs and bowels, you're
there, at the moment of evacuation, to verifiy what I've
kept, what I've expelled... since childhood, since
forever... you control the process... I can count on you...
you won't miss my droppings... I can hear you: *your
mother, here, here I can see a piece you'll have to chew on
again, it doesn't get digested just like that, your Mother's
death, little one, you'll have to make more of an effort...
you've got to absorb life properly... chew on your childhood a
bit more... but there's still a big piece left... so, let's start
again...* and me, I ruminate, me, I hurl into my paunch
and my pate, I come back thirty-six hours later with a

dream, to prove to you that the gastric sugars are starting to work... I shit out signifiers for you, and then you're happy, never too happy, but still a little bit, enough for us to carry on a while longer... *we'll end here for today...*

Right, yeah, me, I'm ending here, for today, I'm done.

Three

OK, SO IT wasn't a great idea. Two nights ago I stuffed
my feeble body full of alcohol and meds. It wasn't very
smart. And when I puked in the night and the Crackpot
rushed out of his room to help me, talking to me about
Mother's decomposition in the cemetery, I regretted it,
really regretted it. I'm not going to get rid of him like
this, the idiot! And when my daughter cried and I could
barely get up to offer her some consolation, curl her into
my arms, I didn't find myself particularly clever.

I ask for forgiveness and give thanks to God for
having spared me, for not having put me to sleep for
good in the odourless exhalations of my little pills. I
don't want to commit suicide. I don't want my body to
rot like Mother's. I'm not calling death. The great circus
must go on, but barking with the wolves. And especially
no mixing. Just the antidepressants. Nothing more.
I'll put myself on Effexor, three times a day, 75mg. At
meal times. I'm calming down. I must behave myself
and speak to my shrink about my death drive. He'll
have a hard-on, without a doubt. The Venlafaxine will
help. I just want to stop dreaming, to stop producing
morbidity. I'll clean the night strewn with corpses which
have been rocking it since childhood. I'm making peace,

beating a retreat, seeking cover, betraying myself.

While the Crackpot was in the next room wildly
confabulating with a group of cohorts he picked
up in some alley, I set about frenetically looking up
the numbers of several loopy clairvoyants, augurs or
marabouts a receptionist at the hospital had given to me
on the sly. There, each more so than the other repeats
that Dr. Forget is going off the rails, but the gossip, the
rumours in the hallways, and the mines full of innuendo
don't affect me. Fuck them all, assholes. I'll make peace
with them too, I'll raise the white flag. Where did I
put that list? I have to hurry up. I'm working at the
hospital at six o'clock and I can't find the directory
of fortune tellers, that was right here on my bed. Oh!
Here it is! I start to dial the number, and of course, I
get the machine. One can't be in too much of a hurry...
Do the spiritualists want for me to die slowly, little by
little, from the great sorrow of having lost Mother, from
the paralyzing fear of being as insane as my brother?
Maybe they want to see me croak. Another answering
machine... Can't these cretins divine that I'm trying to
call? They're really not very clever at their jobs! It's a
conspiracy, and the Crackpot who's expounding twaddle
in the other room to his degenerate friends who stink
of shit in a three kilometre radius and are emptying
my bottles of scotch, are they going to shut it, pariah,
so that I can hear the exalted voice of my future? The

56

mad socialize, they form packs and stick together, they joke around, rattle on in every language, they jest and suddenly it all turns serious again, they gauge the economic situation and proffer opinions. I've thought of everything that's happening to me. I can't bug my shrink again. I have four sessions a week. I'm worn out from telling my story. I need someone to talk to me, to make me promises. Will my brother's friends shut up already? I'm pathetic for letting myself be overrun like this. I eliminate several names from this bloody list. I cross out, I strike through. Just hearing the nasal voices recorded for all eternity on the answering machine, I feel like I don't want to be exorcised by those dullards, I'm not in the mood to levitate. I'm not going to play Pythia with the first person who comes along. The limp voices, the gelatinous voices of false priests put to sleep by the purr of the luring machine. No thank you! I'd rather have someone sing me a Freudian lullaby on my downy couch. There must be some hefty clairvoyants in Montréal. They can't all be pansies, somnambulant impostors. Finally, I talk to a specialist, I make an appointment. I eliminated one woman at the outset who doesn't charge enough money. I don't frequent the flea-ridden. I don't go in for discounts. Mother is dead, and me, I'm alive. My bother is nuts and me, I'm an emergency room surgeon. I'm having a nervous breakdown, for sure, but I'm not as crazy as he is. Peace can't come to me so easily. Like all the defeated, I must do penitence, pay reparations. I'm going to visit the clairvoyant as soon as today. At 11 o'clock, when I'm on call. His crib is right near the hospital. His rates are similar to a surgeon's and his voice hasn't a trace of belligerence.

I close the door to my room behind me, and immediately I see one of my brother's friends coming out of my bathroom, an utterly wild look in his eye. He was shooting up. What are these derelicts doing in my house? I'm not the Salvation Army. Several days ago, it was the birthday of one of these wrecks, and while heating up a piece of pizza for myself after coming back from the hospital I heard the baroque group break into some bitter bickering. One of them was howling, shrieking, because he was slicing off his ring finger to give it to the birthday boy. I had to separate everybody, establish a semblance of a peaceful climate, kindly kick them out and finally do a little sewing job on the ring finger that idiot had started to slice. I made my brother promise me he'd get rid of that rabble, go party in the hallways of the emergency ward, or better yet in some alleyway. My house bears no resemblance to a soup kitchen and I don't practise war medicine. And here they are again, but why are they gathered here? I go toward my living room. The Crackpot immediately introduces me to Manfred, the corpse who was exiting my

bathroom, Viola, a thirty-year old girl, her face utterly
undone, a red nose, and Missouri, a toothless, American
friend who appears to have a marvellous skin disease. It
was a case almost worth studying. They each insisted on
shaking my hand, smiling and swaying. Psychosis, drugs
and alcohol are keeping them alive, for some time yet,
and then it's quite possible that all these good people will
disappear all of a sudden, without so much as a word.
Poof! and that will be the end of the Crackpot's little
friends. Loonies quickly lose their footing. The ravages
are staggering. Everything sets about dysfunctioning
subito presto. It all deteriorates... Even faster than a girl
like me.

When Manfred grabs my hand, he holds onto it for
a long time. He lets out a shriek all of a sudden, saying
I look like his dead mother. The other crazies surround
Manfred and start to laugh joyously, touching one
another all over and nodding. Yes, it's very powerful...
It's right there in front of them. The four comrades all
see that I am Manfred's mother, even though they've
never met her... You would think I was in the emergency
room. I'm just a surgeon, I sew life back together. I
can sew that Manfred's mouth shut. With solid thread.
Nothing complicated, but I have no desire to look after
assailed souls, besieged minds. I don't move, I take cover
in my obstinate silence. Manfred can't stop shrieking
and kisses my hand. *Aïe, aïe, aïe. Do you see what I see,*

she's making me into her slave, he yells, the poor man.
And the chorus of pariah with their rejoinder: *Yes, Yes,
we see. Aïe, aïe, aïe.* To mark the occasion, Viola starts a
frenetic dance on my couch. Manfred hears his mother's
voice in my muteness. She is secretly calling him. He
promises to join her in the beyond. She won't have
come for nothing. Around me, they all see nothing but
darkness, but I don't give. Manfred finally lets go of my
hand and becomes afraid of me. There he is, quivering
and drooling in my living room. All his friends have
calmed down and are tending to their habitual folly.
Manfred needs some rest. His mind is embattled. The
others wash their hands of him. They stop all at once.
The crisis is over. Manfred forgets everything and downs
another bottle of rum. My brother smiles at me.

Under other circumstances, I would have been
troubled by this resemblance to a dead old woman,
and this story would have thrown me into a rage. I
would have had a hissy fit and liquidated Manfred on
the spot by attacking him with my verbal shellfire. No
neighbourhood, no shelter can stand up to me, but
since Mother left, and the Crackpot came back, since
I've been bombarding my body with pills, I capitulate,
I accept things as they present themselves, and with
near affability. The medications are marvellous. I see
everything from a great distance. I'm anesthetized,
completely pacified. I don't care about these freaks. Let

them fuck off somewhere else, or even on my rug, if they like. Today, I administered the right doses. Effexor is magnificent, prodigious. My mouth is a bit dry, otherwise nothing too serious. I'm on my way to the hospital, I'm completely relaxed. My episode two nights ago gave me the chance to adjust my doses. I'm sewing with joy. I want to be very meticulous. The stitches excite me.

At 10 P.M., I find myself at the front door of the clairvoyant's building, rue Hôtel-de-Ville. I enter without knocking, as we'd agreed on the telephone, and I sit in the little room to the right, overhearing whispers on the other side of the wall. Whispers, secrets, tenuity, life sliding lecherously in the interstices of signs. It's hot in this room. It feels good in this indescribable, flashy mess, in this familiar place which leaves one speechless. The rustling of a hoarse voice creates a constant little noise behind a door, in the distance. It's the purr of destiny. I hear someone going out. A child appears. He must be eight years old. A kid for whom misfortunes and joys have just been predicted, the *coups de théâtre* and powers of his existence. I want to leave, to leave the shambles-salon of the caster of spells upon children. But Jessy is there smiling in the doorway. I immediately like this black giant from Louisiana, just as the nurse today said I would. A dispatch from the dead, a prophet with clinking charms and bracelets, a fallen angel, fallen from I don't know what sky. Right away I want to follow him, offer him my hand and approach my future that he's almost carrying in his big arms.

His office is there. Mother as well. Jessy sees her right away, when I sit on the wooden chair with which I am firmly presented. He places himself across from me, looks at me for about ten seconds which seem very long, and laconically, simply, says: *Oh! Oh! You brought your mother. Yes, yes. Very good, very, very good, but I charge more for two people. OK?* I agree to his request, desperately searching for Mother with my eyes. I imagine her impishly perched on a bookshelf perhaps, or naughtily hidden between the folds of the vertiginously heavy curtains surrounding the enormous window. I imagine her a child, playing hide-and-seek with my pain, with the dull grief squeezing my entrails. I must stop this game. I'll pay anything, ruin myself for love, liquidate the future so that she will appear. I want her there, even on credit, in the astronomical failure of my absurd reason. I miss her so much, my adored mother, my little violet whom I can no longer make into a bouquet. Even if she were there, he says, I wouldn't see her, I wouldn't see her anymore, I, who spent my life dazzled by the sight of her? Jessy asks me to breathe, to feel my mother. An odour intoxicates me. It's the fragrance of violets that made her into a ghost, before,

when she was alive. I remember having often carried
back in my luggage bottles of that *Acqua di Parma* with
which she spritzed herself her whole life long. The scent
envelops the room, anoints it, cloaks it with morbid,
suave pleasures. I find myself alone with the rose and
violet shadow and the black colossus, this impossible
Jessy who has the power to turn tables, to make mothers
appear and resuscitate time. My mother is here,
magnificent, grandiose, tender and engaging, amplectant
emanation. I'm mad with joy for finding her, my mother
who smells good, past and future. She's sorry for having
let me down, for having wanted the end and even
paradise. *At the end, it's too difficult. One day we seek
death out, we call upon it, we bark, we yap loudly to make
it come.* And yes, it came, and she had to go, and I wasn't
there. I was sewing bodies back together, further down,
in another wing. The hospital is big. And when death
comes along, there's no making it wait. And when death
knocks, you've got to let it knock... My little mother left
quickly, but for her to leave again, she needs my
forgiveness. *You remember when you were a child, I told
you about those mothers in the camps who suffered so much
for being separated from their children. They were made to
die, mothers, children, simply by being torn from one
another. The mothers' last thoughts, in the oven, were
toward that other Medean abyss in which their little ones
died alone, in terror. When I was dying, my Florette, I*

63

thought that one day you would die without me. I never thought I would die, what can you do. I'm a mother. I wanted to throw myself into death, drown there. You know how seductive death is. You've always loved it so. I called death with my whole body. My body amputated of its breasts and then of the rest, everything else. It was fulgurating. You remember... Your colleague the surgeon who operated on me told you I was rotten through and through. You cried. You came to report back to me, the words of your imbecilic colleague. We laughed. You told me everything. We would laugh at the slightest thing. I desired death, I wanted to lose myself in it, to stop suffering. Cancer hurts. Such suffering! A real horror. You blamed yourself as you watched me suffer for having been so harsh with your dying, disembowelled patients. Because it's true that we suffer. It's unbelievable how much. Death arrived in the night and I asked to be carried off. I told myself it wouldn't come through again so soon. I didn't want to miss my ride. But I was only thinking of my children. A person can't change. We're mothers... I was dying alone, but I thought only of you. I told myself one day you would die without me. And I blamed myself, terribly, my little girl from Auschwitz, lost in a world where everything is a cutting. You don't like cuttings, Flore. You stitch, you stitch, and you found that my sutures weren't good. That they would leave scars. You told off your pig of a colleague. But I'm dead and there are no more scars. I feel good where I am, in the mauve, in the pink. Death is a colour. Nothing more. A bit of a sad colour verging on violet. I'm fine up there. I can't explain it to you. At least there is no more death. What a relief! I'm not afraid of leaving you anymore, of not seeing you grow up, that a misfortune will befall us. For me, it's over. A very long rest. Forgive me, Flore, for not having been a mother to the end. I abandoned you, my big white girl. But I couldn't take much more. I was sick of the cancer, of that fulgurating, fast-forwarding thing. Galoping death catching up with us. We want it to win and to be done with it. I thought only of myself. I hope you aren't too angry at me. What will you do with your failing mother, the mother who takes off, the mother who doesn't know anymore, who shrieks at death. All of a sudden, death comes, and it's good that way. As though a happiness at last. It's good to be able to close one's eyes and not be afraid anymore. I left you, my Flore. It must be that I loved death, that I desired it even more than to remain among my kids. When you were small, I had that bad accident while on vacation in France. I was driving at top speed along a road in Normandy. And bang! In the ditch! Almost in death. You never forgave me. You were so resentful of my travelling without you. Little, you were cannibal, piranha, my carnivorous flower. I always had to be near you, loving you, stroking you. You were a tyrant, Flore, even as a child! You would have eaten me alive! There were voices in your head even before you began speaking. The doctors said: tinnitus and auditory hallucinations. They examined your ears or your throat and it was like a radio. Hertzian waves. But you, you said it was your internal voice, your intimate voice, your Tourette's syndrome, voices that fuse, that castigate, that shriek, catapulting voices. Terrible voices, but you got along well with them. You're a monster, Flore. You're hard as stone. But I loved you that way. I alone knew how to remove all your asperities. I washed you clean of evil. You ate from my hands, after hours of struggle and strife, of course. You could concede nothing. And when I had my accident, you blamed me for having thought of leaving you alone on the other side of the Atlantic, that terrible sea, its water raging against our family, unstitched, strewn across the beaches. The drunken and violent Atlantic that we tamed from Caen to Montréal, from your Grandmother's to our rue Lajoie. That's all that was left. Our water crossings. Do you remember, my Flore, how overwhelmed you were by the Pacific? You went quite late in life. At the age of thirty-two. Me, I never so much as put the tip of my foot nor a toe into your idyllic Pacific. The Atlantic was enough for me. I didn't travel anymore. Just between two shores. Caen-Montréal. But you called me from your hotel in Montecino, and had me listen to the waves breaking beneath your feet. You said: "Mother, you know, the world is big and I think that here, I could forget you. Here, I could have another mother... Yes, I could." You were crying, Flore. "I'm coming back, I'm coming back right now. Mother, there's only the

Atlantic, there's only you. I'm coming." You returned there often. Bora Bora, Hawaii, the Virgin Islands, Australia, New Zealand. You were swallowing the Pacific. You wanted to sink into it and emerge armed for a new life. Venus Anadyomene. You tried to detach yourself from me. To find yourself another ocean. To make yourself into a fish, a whale. You always loved me too much, Flore, but without considering me. You wanted to devour me, to cannibalize me. Luckily, I stood up for myself. Your brothers went to live elsewhere. Florent left, yes, but did he live? Only Genêt pulled through the mad love that flowered in you, in the three of you, my children. I don't know what was in me that put you into such a state. A smell, you said. That Violette de Parme fragrance, my namesake brand. A scent, not that of a woman, no, that of a mother. I was a mother. I always liked being a soil in which you could grow happily. Your brothers didn't want any part in it, and you, you stayed and made cuttings on human bodies. You blamed me, Flore, at the time of my accident. You didn't speak to me for months, and you told me that at that moment, if I were to die again, you would never forgive me. That I would have to kill you first, that I should smother you in your sleep or put a violent poison into your breakfast. The nonsense, the exaggerations of my big girl, Flore Forget... But your childish blackmail made its way in me. It had an effect on me. I found that I was denied any death. I saw that I was eternal for you. As one grows old, you know, one often wants to die. Life is sometimes too long. Life is literally used up. One wants to lie down and never open one's eyes again. Throw oneself into a hole and never grow back. In the last years, it all became heavy. But I told myself that you needed your Mother, your birth soil, that my old uterus could still greet you. Madness in my thinking, Flore, because with you, everything goes mad. You ruin everything. But with me, you never managed to make our love rotten. I prevented you from doing so. I was nothing but patience, nothing but attentiveness. You weren't able, Flore, and that's why you loved me so much. With me, you couldn't play your little comedy of death. In me, you found your meaning again, you grew, Flore, my Flore, so white, so white in your maternal soil. And your pacific flights, your flights toward the other mother signalled your infinite return to me, to your mother's belly. I was the one toward whom you went. It's not my fault, my girl. That's how it was between us. I didn't want to keep you. I didn't want to have you to myself. You know it. I wanted to return to France and even be buried there. To be done with the crossings, my fantastic straddlings of too big an ocean. But you made me into a sun and became a heliotrope. Always turned toward me even in your betrayals. Do you know how to betray, Flore? I don't think you do. Just like you don't understand life. You want it to lie down at your feet, for it to make itself beautiful, for it to eat from your hand. I stayed here. For you, so that you wouldn't be alone. And I asked that my body be laid in the

Côte-des-Neiges cemetery. I gave up on the flowers of February on my renewed grave, I gave up on a flowering Easter. I am buried beneath the snow, and there are nothing but dandelions in that damn cemetery, and I'm not eating them. I'm too proud for that. I know flowers too well. You're a surgeon, my girl. For you, life is an operating room in which you are in control of everything. And as far as body openers go, it doesn't get better than you. You are by far the best. Everyone wants to have their entrails seen by Dr. Forget. But for crying out loud, Flore, your dog is demonic, your cat eats on the table and you don't domesticate anything. You can't do it... I offered you my grave. You'll go collect yourself there and you'll bring me marvellous bouquets, breathtaking sprays, reseda, because you know how to pick it. But winter is so long and your flowers freeze fast, they fly off into the winds of January and sweep the alleyways. The employees warned you. Flowers must be planted. We're in cold country, a violent country. But you come along with your extravagant flowers and send them packing, those men who gesticulate and sometimes even yell beside my grave brandishing a shovel. You send them packing, just as they are. You predict their cancer and months at the hospital and if, by misfortune, they happen to fall on you, you'll take out their prostatic tumor in pain. And they're afraid, those big strapping men who know the dead and their secrets. They retreat, cowards that they are, before your strident cries, your Greek Pythian cries, doctor

69

of misfortune, a diagnostician of the worst! Then you burst into tears on my still fresh grave and you apologise to me, saying that your medications aren't properly dosed, that psychoanalysis is so difficult, that you miss me so much, that you want to calm down, yes, let life pass, not even gesture toward it, stop hearing voices, the voices that turn to air currents in your four-winds mind. You don't want to suffer anymore, you don't want to keep tilting, my Don Quixote of a daughter, at windmills. That's what you're telling me through your terrifying cries that twist your face into grotesque grimaces. And then you explode, ask me to come back. Why have I abandonned you, you and little Rose? Why a dead grandmother, for my darling little granddaughter, my sparkling girl? Why life without me, life without the love that kept us alive, and that is only yours to give now? No, I didn't wait for you. You had gone out for a moment and I wanted to be done with it. If you had been there, you wouldn't have let me go. I made the most of it. I seized the opportunity. Death doesn't come by very often, you've got to make do. What I mean is that death came, and I left. The way one leaves with a lover, one quivering day. I took off, Flore, and I knew you would go mad, but the cancer was ravaging my body and my mind. My cancer was cheating everything. My breasts and my thorax, my liver and then my spleen, the larger intenstine, and then the smaller one. My brain was splitting. I was already losing my sight. My breath was smothering me. My bones gnawing at my flesh. I was already dead all over and death came. And wanted me. You found me lifeless, you stayed a while, drunk against my body. And then you quickly returned to your battle against death so that it wouldn't triumph over everything, especially not you. When you were small, you were already telling death off. You confronted it, insulted it. Death was your enemy. You wouldn't take it. Death could come. It would find you self-assured. You became a surgeon to ring its neck. But let it be known, my girl, that I loved death, that I wanted it, I called it, I summoned death to me. I was languishing for death. I abandoned you. I'm no longer a mother, I'm nothing at all. I'm dead, Flore, dead and well buried. You were there, all three of you, to put me in the earth, in the soil of Québec, which only allows for flowers a very brief time of the year. You must grant the dead their end. You must go on, and on that night, you were right to save that life that asked only to be. You must love life, Flore, and everything will flourish again.

My mother disappears, Jessy tells me so. He becomes quiet, absent, he has nothing left to say. My mother disappears, asking me to abandon her to her death. Jessy walks me to the door and I ask him several questions. He doesn't remember a thing, he leant his voice, his soil, his office to something unknown to him. This story has no witnesses. Mother appeared only to me.

I have to go to the cemetery to see her grave again,

on this glacial night at the beginning of winter. Mother visited me. It's my turn to go see her. In the car, it's violently cold. Mother's burial comes back in my memory. Those are the hours that flower in me again in the discomfort of my car on the icy road of December.

At Mother's funeral, the church was in celebration, the church was flowering. It was wonderfully beautiful on that Easter Tuesday, a few short days after Mother's death on Good Friday. The nave was bursting with bouquets and the crosses and columns were crumbling beneath the flowers. These were springtime joys. The joys of a summer announcing itself. Our nostrils were full of it. Life wanted to infiltrate itself into us. Beneath the feverish, exciting odor of the tuberoses, the lilacs and magnolias, my two brothers carried the coffin out of the church, with the help of several friends. And we disappeared into the limousine. I could see Florent gesticulate up front, beside the driver, wriggling every which way. He was speaking loudly and clearly. A tinted window separated us. We arrived at the cemetery. The sun was hot. We crossed the alleys between the graves.

The coffin filled the hole dug for it that very morning. The hole was enormous. The violet coffin, which seemed heavy and difficult to manoeuver, was to be planted there. A bulb of the future was being interred. I insisted on tossing a fistful of dirt on it. Plock! It made a dry sound. A little irritating sound.

Rose wanted to do the same. My brothers followed.
Everything knocked against Mother's coffin, but
she didn't answer. Not a word, not a sound. She was
being buried. In August, she would be there. Summer
grows fast. The sun was blinding us. Florent stood
for a moment near the hole, as though he were a tree
attempting to root himself there. His big mass of
flesh cast some shadow on the coffin exposed to the
unexpected sun of March. I read on the gravestone the
words which Mother herself had had written before her
death. "Everything dies. Everything flowers again." And
underneath: "Everything flowers again. Everything dies."
I had a bit of a laugh. I laughed because Mother only
conceived of the world in terms of shoots, cuttings and
shrubs. Mother was the philosopher in the garden or the
greenhouse. Rose was becoming heavy in my arms, and
her legs anxiously gripped my hips. Florent disappeared.
His body hurtled through the forest of tombs. I could
only see his head bobbing above the crosses. Then the
sun blinded me terribly. He was gone when I opened
my eyes again. We took the path to Mother's house.
There, a celebration awaited us. The air was joyous. I
remember having thought that I was happy. It must have
been a hard day, a battering day. Mother was dead. But
everything was over. Peace would come one day.

It's Mother's funeral that comes back to me this
December evening when I had almost forgotten it,

swallowed up, drowned in the troubled waters of my artificial narcosis. The gate to the garden of the dead is sealed shut. At the cemetery, there's no entry. The disappeared are sound asleep, and in winter, the earth rocks them, singing the song of a springtime that won't come again.

I go back to work. While parking my car in my reserved spot, I wonder why flowers aren't eternal. They wilt, deteriorate, decompose vivaciously. The stars, the planets, the stones, the rocks resist, and even the shooting stars struggle magnificently against the usury of time. We must invest in what endures, in what will still be standing in three hundred and fifty million years. The dead are right to want to be stone, to make themselves into tombs. They want to topple into eternity. As flowers they wilt too quickly. As a child, at La Malbaie, at my grandfather Forget's, planted in front of the awkward river, the river cracking with ice, rending itself with groans, I could see those large rocks riveted to the beach, and the very arrogant stone, so present, there, after and before us. Humans and flowers rot, every day.

A voice shrieks into the hospital loudspeaker as I push heavily against the door. *Dr. Flore Forget's presence is urgently requested in operating room C-8034. Dr. Flore Forget. Wah, wah, wah.* It's life ephemeral that's calling. The life I prolong, the life that wants to flourish again. It's life, some kind of whore, calling me for help. I come

74

running. I'm there... You know it.

Four

IT SEEMS TO me I have loved before. I mean Love.
Loving someone other than my dead, decomposing
mother, sticky and repulsive with death. It seems to me
I have desired before, loudly and clearly and dreadfully.
It seems to me I've been in pain before. Lots of pain.
Ow, ouch, stop! Don't you see... I've really suffered.
Like a beast. Like an animal at slaughter. I've known
amputation. I cut out what was rotting my life. I'm
a surgeon. I know how to trim when necessary, yes, I
know what to do. With composure and dexterity. I've
saved my skin in extremis. It was minus one. How well
I work! Great artistry. The stitches are barely visible.
It's my specialty. At the hospital, I'm known for that,
for beautiful sutures, invisible scars, meticulousness
with needles and surgical thread. My very own way of
stapling flesh together. A je-ne-sais-quoi in ligature.
And as with my patients, I operated. It was a long time
ago, at least ten years, twenty years, thirty years. I don't
know anymore. Of course I'm exaggerating. Only by
way of exaggeration can anything be said. Only excess
is capable of accounting somewhat for horror. It was
a hundred years ago, and then life goes fast, so fast.
It carries on, it turns. The events suddenly become

blurred. You can't see anything anymore... You still feel pain nonetheless. But you don't really remember what's causing all the pain. You know it's terrible, but there are opiates, panaceas of drugs, there's work, the hatred of one's neighbour, weeping, pleading patients: it keeps you busy. It's crazy how it can keep you busy, and I've always kept myself busy. No one's succeeded in killing me. But honestly it isn't for lack of trying. Perhaps they lacked determination.

Love, there's no telling, it's viscous. It's really filthy. I was rejected, turned out, cheated on, cuckolded, lied to, but always with a smile. Me, I couldn't see anything. I was moving forward with my eyes closed, I was moving forward like a modern Tiresias who envisioned the future while missing all his prophecies. It was through me and me alone that my misfortune arrived. I told myself that it would change, that it would come, that it was because of resistance, numbness, hibernation, powerlessness in the face of life. But I was prepared to fight. Life, for me, was a hand-to-hand combat, I cut its throat in no time flat. Obstacles, I eliminated them, warrior that I am.

I have loved. That's how it's said. So I said it. And even in the present. Something like: "I love you". A whisper, a cry, a howl, a yap at the moon. *I love you, ooh, ooh, ooh!* There. That was enough... The world had to render itself docile, life had only to keep itself in check.

I was going to hold up hope, steal happiness, shoot rotten luck, gun down my misery. Sure, I misstepped, I mean royally. Magesterially. Sumptuously. I've got all the qualities of a falling queen. I'm a grand dame. It's true I fell, divine, angelic, marmoreal, from on high. Sometimes I still wanted to applaud, because it's not every day you see belly flops like mine. I'm not afraid of anything, granted. I'm not half-assed, that's for certain. I wiped out, I busted myself up. It's a good thing I'm a body patcher!

Yes, I have loved before. Madly, passionately, and then not at all, because you become disgusted with yourself, with such filth, because it tears your heart out, it gives you nausea. I regret only one thing: not having killed. Yes, that, I do regret. Even with time. Killing isn't bad. It's not what people think. It calms, it cleans. Shedding blood purifies life a little bit. It's tragic, pathetic, romantic and malevolent. And evil must be wrung out. One cannot simply think that it's good or noble to move on to the next thing, that time will do its work. I should have been less petty. I should have blown up the guts of my history one day in a bloodbath. I should have disembowelled it, gutted it, eviscerated it. Left the squalid, the foul, for dead. And by the spilled blood, washed clean the detritus. And by proffered death, offered myself freedom. I'm decidedly ungenerous. Ragged, reticent, ratatouille with

cowardice, I didn't make the move, hadn't the breadth,
the mettle. A good stab between the shoulder blades, or
better yet straight through the heart. I'm a doctor, after
all, I know where to strike... I should have pierced the
abscess, given in to the accident. My car rolling along,
dragging the remains. A torso shoved brutally into the
hole, into the precipice of life. A meal seasoned with the
salts of death. A blood red vodka swallowed sexually. A
pillow smothered against nostrils snoozing with orgasms.
Organs sliced among the hot caresses of the bath. A
whitewashed wall beneath which the living dead pain
is rendered mute. Gouged eyes neglectfully unsponged.
Violent illnesses inoculated with giant doses, AIDS, good
and fresh, slowly penetrating, black syphilis purchased
at a discount, voracious spiders with forgotten names,
venomous fish that kill with their tongues. A stupefying
explosion that sends kilometres worth of intestines
into the gutter. I could have been a great murderer...
Followed the example of the kamikazes, made horror
my creature. It seems I lacked will. And imagination. I
wanted death, but I didn't even know whose anymore.
Mine, theirs? It was all a pulp. I remained incapable of
articulating assassinating words, criminal phrases, of
bestowing wrath and constructing hatred. I waited for
it to pass, and then it passed. I left a lot behind. More
skin, more bowels, little factoried chickens with friable
bones. Nothing left of the hard ass no one dares mess

with. *Insipid, sweetie,* that's what I'd tell myself. Happily, there were green sauces, red sauces, to give me a bit of flavour. I was chewy, inedible, foul, all boiled tendons, trembling gelatine. I should have assassinated, sacrificed, sent everything to hell. Not thought of forgiveness or absolution, but instead seen everything in red and sanguinary ablutions. Made a rabbit stew of her flesh. I should have made a meal out of it, the main course, all cut up into pieces, swallowed, gulped down the tough bits, but digested none of it. I should have set fire to the city and the house, destroyed what had been touched and razed impurity. I should have shaved the head of my restive shame, marched it across the public square. My name in the newspapers, face plastered on the front page and arms on page two. "Surgeon knew how to cut up cadaver". "The butcher of the Plateau made minced meat of it". I should have caused a scandal. I should have warned someone when the police arrived, turned on the gas and blown the whole neighbourhood to bits. I should have imagined him in the arms of his mistress. Understood that he was quietly ploughing her lean vagina while lending her my name. Should have blown his hollow brains out on the night of a full moon; in the surging discharge of a love too brutal.

You scare me, I've heard it said. *You scare me, you're capable of anything.* Well, yeah, and even of forgetting you. Flore forgets you but she never forgives. *You scare*

81

*me with your lunatic head, you give me the creeps with
your head that invents things, your head that creates stories,
makes quite a film for itself! You see me jiggling my bobble
with the feet of defenseless little lambs in stirrups, with
near virgin little girls I'm deflowering. It's totally absurd,
my little sprig, and you know it, but I don't know why
you insist on hurting yourself, Flore, my mimosa, my little
springtime heather. It's the trade, it's the job of meeting
women, girls, and spreading their legs. You don't fornicate
with the guy who's split open his large intestine. It's the same
thing... Vaginas, uteruses, it's just my workplace. What a
racket inside your noggen! You're really making this into a
merry-go-round, a big carousel! You shouldn't be a surgeon,
my poppy, you should be writing scripts for X-rated films.
You make me laugh, my flower. Come on, smile for me? But
you're making such a face, my lilly-of-the-valley!*

    You scare me, so he said, when he came back from
the hospital that evening as I let it be known, while
chopping up a rabbit, that if he didn't split immediately,
I'd also cut him up into tiny pieces in the night without
killing him first. I'd fry him up in the pan. While
packing his suitcase he even started up again with
rumours he had heard at medical school, the school of
cadavers, that I was already considered morbid and that
I inflicted the worst kind of torture on the dead. I was
the savage one, the anthropophagist. My teeth grew in
the night with my scalpel. *You scare me, you've always*

been violent, and Isabelle told me that you threated her this morning on the telephone. You're completely nuts. Well, you haven't seen anything yet. *Keep talking, my rabbit,* that's what I kept saying to him...

It seems I have loved before and it's true I was crazy, but only crazy for you, and then for our insanity. It seems to me that love was something, like a world that's a little too big, like a heart that overflows and hemorrhages. *I'm leaving you,* so he said. *I'm leaving you. People are afraid of you. You've got the face of a dug-up corpse and you're completely nutso.* He was packing his bags. He was basking in meanness, in the division of goods, in the separation between mind and body, and me, I was chopping the rabbit. It's the only thing I can do right, cut up meat. Don't forget your speculums, you can't take anything with you to paradise. Before you know it, you'll have counted your losses, you'll have slept with the director of the hospital and when she's done, she'll toss you out, like the others, like a piece of shit. Then you'll understand that I've been to see her to tell her that you were going through a hard time, that you were a good guy and she absolutely had to take care of you. And you, you fell for it, and I didn't have to put up with you coming on to the cunts in the hospital corridors, you with your cowardly mug, your little mug that plays the *I no longer recognise you when I see you, you're too demented* game with me. Yeah, the director

83

showed you the straight and narrow, the way to the door.

That Madeleine Lévesque is a right bitch, but she has a way with old yobs like you. She tosses you out quickly and cleans up afterward. She cures and curetages. A big swob of the deck. Flip, flop. Madelaine Lévesque is a psychiatrist, and I can tell you she comes from a powerful race. You don't want to mess with them. You've been festering for years in a pathetic hospital having to perform obstetrics. You give birth to tadpoles. It's far less glamourous than unblocking tubes in single file or doing vaginal bypass surgery to your heart's content. Madeleine Lévesque got you good. What can you do... She sleeps with all the Slavs at the hospital and then annihilates them for fear of being dumped by them. You had your share, that's for sure, and then I forgot. You, yes, I forgot about you, your existence.

It seems I have loved before. But it couldn't have been you. It was like a mirage, a ghost of happiness, a hallucination. You were making me suffer with your past, with your little smile, your matrimonial curriculum vitae and your exes that taunted me with so much dexterity. I was suffering your usury. Your second-hand life, your threadbare stories and your feigned silence that didn't speak volumes. I was suffering under the weight of what cannot be erased, which you would never have helped me to carry. I thought I was Atlas. The

world was so heavy... On the day of the rabbit, I forgot
everything. I cooked it up with mustard, the kind that
stings your nose, and chewed it well. It went: Ahhh! I
stopped the pain, closed the taps. I sent my life into an
old dumpster, a big orange bag, and I tied a big knot.
I never saw your three daughters to whom I'd given a
good licking. Apparently, they despise me... I wrecked a
home! They're still friends with some of your mistresses,
colleagues of their mother's who didn't suspect a thing.
But everyone shut up, and it's been so long... Hatred
is only for me. I forget but I never forgive. I don't say
hello, not even good-bye, and especially not thank you,
and I don't pretend you're an exquisite being. You're
still cheating on your wife, the latest one, still fresh.
You're still cheating on your sweetheart despite the
hard-hitting years that will crush you, jackhammer you.
You really don't grow old! It's insane how young you
look... So when you sent flowers for Mother's funeral, I
immediately had your tasteless wreath redirected to the
address of your flea-ridden gynecological office on the
north side of the city. You must have decorated your
clinic with it. You never throw anything away. But then,
a mortuary crown must blend in well with the walls of
your lugubrious life, of your medical cubbyhole where
sad and abandoned women lay themselves out. Unless
you took the whole shebang home to give it to your
young wife who will happily receive the crumbs of my

existence and my mother's. You didn't like my mother.
You couldn't stand her. She couldn't take your accent
and more than anything she doubted your abilities as a
doctor. You dished out so much bull about menopause
that you undermined what might have remained of
your credibility. What a terrible idea to have sent those
flowers! Mother was a florist, I don't know whether you
remember. So your four barely white lillies, awkwardly
stuck into a clump of green moss in the shape of a
crown wasn't going to impress us, we, the children of a
Violette. You went to see Mother after the Rose's birth,
to let her know that you were the father. You never did
know how to count... It had already been four years
since I'd played the the rabbit trick... With you, I was
just a sterile, unwatered soil, arid, dried up land, a
barren girl, a braying girl. *You've got to have an abortion,
my blossom, if ever it happens to you. My daughters aren't
old enough, we're so good just like this. Later, it will come.
Naturally. I'll help it pass if your delay persists, if the blood
doesn't appear, if the English don't deign turn up, if the
poppies' heads don't dart up, if the catamenia continues to
sulk. I'm a gynecologist, my red one, I'll sort you out. Don't
worry whatever you do. That's what I'm here for.* With you,
I was a stuffed duck, an owl plugged with straw and
fodder, a wilted bouquet, good and dry, a decomposed
pot-pourri, fallen to dust. A thousand little pieces on
the rug quickly swept up, that's what I'd become. A pile

of dessicated particles, a pile of sheep that don't even
bleat anymore and for I don't know how long, twigs of
nothingness pulverised in an instant, a little mountain of
ash and debris, a trifle never trifled with, to avoid getting
dirty... And you never got dirty. *I'm a gynecologist, I work
with stench,* you would say, kissing my neck. That's as
low as you could go, you didn't like smells. That's how I
understood, acting like a bloodhound, a snorting doggie,
that there was another woman. A diabolical aroma,
that's what I was smelling all day long. The fragrance
of your amorous and chemical decompositions. I had
olfactory indigestion. I was your Flore, your flourish,
the one whose emanations you loved, whose bouquet
you desired. Give me a break... Love, a fetid and foul-
smelling stink. A stench that makes me want to puke. I
hadn't seen anything, hadn't sussed anything. I thought
we loved one another. I thought, you and me, that we
were destined to be together. But I was a buzzard, a
brainless beast. I'll never forgive myself for being an ass,
a silly goose, an ostrich, a stuffed turkey. I was in deep
do-do. I was taking a piss in the begonias. I discovered
the pot of roses. One day, in a conversation: a click in
my head and all of a sudden, there it was. I could sense
the demon by his smell in all of your movements. All
of a sudden I could see the precise shade of rose with
which I had daubed my life. I understood the trips, the
delays, the smiles, the kisses, the desires. I grasped the

origin of my dishonest life in which I played the humble seamstress of hope and intestines. My life as a miserable maidservant, a consenting victim.

I think I have loved. At least those five years. That was an eternity ago, and how long it was... It is a time that doesn't pass, a time that stays caught in my throat, a time that fills me with dread, and makes me give up the ghost. I think I have loved. But how can I be certain of it? We experience vile things and then we forget them. We sometimes wonder whether we didn't invent them. I needed to write myself a love. And it was yours, and it was ours. But already I was lying, already, I was filling the void. I think that I have loved before. I wanted a life. Well, I had one! And I'm a weakling, for sure, but never in front of you. A weakling before time, a weakling before blood, before the smothering and the madness of being alive. A weakling incapable of telling a woman that her child is dead, swallowed by the night. That flesh is suffering, damaged, annihilated, raped in its very breath, killed in its sighs. That being alive is a kind of ridicule.

I wasn't made for surgery, not for announcements, omens, messages and embassies of death. Who will save me? Not love, that's for sure... I continue to sew this facticious smile into my face, and I make myself small so that destiny will forget about me. It could be worse. My mother wasn't young. My daughter remains very much alive. She gets on my nerves and adores her uncle, that Crackpot who insinuates himself and makes my decisions. Love can be remade and the world continues. Sure, I can suffer. But not too much. I require it. The pills are there. I mustn't exaggerate, make too much of it, amplify, bluff or embroider... I'm done bragging about holding the key to misfortune. I have a dead Mother who is moldering at the cemetery. She has a burial place: it's a haven. There is worse than us. I can go weep on her fresh grave, I can make gardens out of the neighbourhood, flower the tombs. There's enough to keep me busy. Everything grows in the neighbourhood. It's still very fertile. Life always takes up again. May fresh grass grow and may blossoms bloom! May the world run, may it rush toward tomorrow! I'm happy with what I've got. I'm growing myosotis, the plant of love, the mouse's ear, *ne-m'oubliez-pas,* forget-me-nots. I'm turning the tomb blue. Mother loved the colour and she loved flowers, and she doesn't love anymore at all, and nothing more than anything, and most of all not me.

I'm all about cuttings or horticulture. I know the meristem and the vascular cambium. I can care for flowers, graft anything you want, but I can't splice a bit of remaining mother, I can't give myself the love I no longer have. I only know how to cut. I'm a great exciser. I take your pain away. Love, I can only make it grow. And I remain good and lonely and rage isn't even my

lecherous companion anymore. I remind myself that at
the beginning, you and I spoke of our funerals. The first
time, after the first kiss, after having inhaled the insane
fragrance of your hair so brown, after having touched
with the tip of my soul the sky and the blue of your eyes
for the first time, and we were already talking about
the end. In love's bosom, we did the rounds of time,
perched on the great needles of the most most imaginary
clocks, we were already quivering at the horror of the
brevity of days, and dizzy, drunken, we mastered the
last moments with serenity. We wanted tombs on the
heights of mount Royal, we wanted views on the future.
I could see rose coloured flowers at my funeral and a
large, well padded coffin. And you were galant, you let
me die first and despite my young age. You came quickly
to join me, you couldn't live without me. Mother had
the rose and the padding, such was her will, and the
magnificent grave at the top of the cliff. From there, she
can see the city, and me, I see the emptiness I want to
throw myself into on each little visit. I had to respect
her last wishes. A large coffin that will take years to
decompose. Magnificently gay satin, a superb rose, and
the salmon dress she wanted to wear on big nights out,
her disproportionate rovings. Everything you need to
leave this world in style, when you die like a packet
of bones, barely recognisable. Cancer is cannibalistic,
but no more than worms. I would like not to have

followed Mother's orders, I would like not to have been the upstanding, obediant daughter who agreed to bury the body of her mother and who wakes in the night dreaming of maggots. I would like not to have been that loving daughter who says yes to her Mother, who only ever said yes to her. I never married. I never left Mother. You, you were meant to marry me, but I stood you up. At night, without the meds, I'm always with her. I'm rotting and decomposing. I wake up bathed in a cold sweat, I suffocate. But honestly, Mother, did you think of me? Why did you refuse to be burned so barely alive, annihilated presto, to have your bones roasted and your meat grilled? Why didn't you want to make the inferno yours and never mind death? Why didn't you want to become dust again at top speed, you who drove so fast in your new Mercedes? Why didn't you want to accelerate the time of death, quicken the future, for it to be as it would be in a hundred or even two thousand years, for dust to be dust, for nothingness to be itself? It's horrible to live with the dead, not the abstract dead, not the historic dead, but the dead I know, the dead in fresh earth, the dead with flowering tombs, the dead, labourers of decomposition. Love and humans are the decomposed.

Mother, let me tell you, you're a dirty bitch. You thought only of yourself, of your salmon dress, of your funereal hairdo, the fragrance of your flowers. You had made all the arrangements, I had only to follow orders, but you hadn't imagined that I might suffer, that we'd think of you, the Crackpot and me. You're not Snow White in her glass shrine, nor saint Bernadette whom I saw in her windowed coffin one day in Nevers, Nevers, in France, where I caught the mad fear of death and my ideas about love. Mother, you had taken me there, do you remember, to visit the saint. I saw the crippled, the infirm, the blind and the paralytics. I saw the crutches, the shoes, the limbs that grow back and the faith that amplifies, but I never liked seeing the dead woman, the dead woman at Nevers, where she doesn't rot. You found her so beautiful, Mother, your Bernadette in flowers; you left her a magnificent bouquet and begged of her that she protect us... At Nevers, Mother, life was intact. Everything smelled of the tomb, but you, you were smiling, and proudly, you showed me the force of your faith: Bernadette, superb in her burial gown, mummified with pomp and tragedy, and happy. And me, I didn't want to look at her, your devout lover, your friend the beatific. Didn't want to see her so peaceful in death, as in her aura. I had asked to go out and puked for a long time on the phantom limbs of the fervent legless cripples, on the blue chasubles of the sisters of the Trinity who were emerging from a yellow bus giving a hand to the dying. It was a beautiful day in Nevers, in France, and, Mother, you were showing me

your beloved country. This wasn't Normandy and cow
dung, but it was a little bit Lourdes, the Bernadette
in Nevers, near the bus and the stinking vomit that I
attempted, with application, to eject from my spindly
child's body that didn't even eat... Mother, you probably
have no recollection, in your world of forgetting, of
your beatific Bernadette, your saint in clogs... You had
so much love for her clean, well-polished tomb, and
me, I was so terrified of smiling death. You wanted to
be like her, like that foolish, blessed girl from beyond
who solicits a bit of heaven and knows how small she is
beside her God. You wanted to be Thérèse of Lisieux,
the miracle maker, the great sacrificed woman who
adored her father. And you wanted me to love her,
the insipid one in her glass coffin, the sleeping beauty
who never wakes. Well, I vomitted everything that day.
And then, Mother, you know, death isn't like that. I
can tell you that it smells bad. I became a doctor, I saw
Maccabees, saints, maybe, sure, you never know, but
also black souls. In death, everyone is the same colour,
except for those who smoked. God recognises them,
but it's all he sees. Blackened organs and consuming
time. I became a doctor, Mother, so as not to be afraid
of death's signal, of radiant death that has such airs of
kindliness. I became a doctor so as to autopsy your
mummified Bernadette! I opened the stomach of your
dead, and I thought that was it, that I knew everything

and that I was no along afraid, least of all the dead. But I was mistaken. How stupid I was! I hadn't seen your death, Mother, true death, the death to come, and all the forced cadavers take away nothing of my pain and the hurt of being alive. I miss you, Mother. So many things to do... We spoke every night, but I told you nothing. We had not yet spoken, and I certainly hadn't told you about Nevers-in-coffin and the good sisters who picked me up when I was wading in my white vomit. We spoke of everything and even of necessity, but it must be that speaking isn't very easy, especially when there is so much love between us. Mother, you loved your saint, and with you, I wanted to adore her. In my own way, of course, by seeing her alive. I don't like dead women, that's why it's so hard to continue to love you. Of Normandy, I remember the strong smell of fields and animals: cows and pigs and overripe camembert that I spread on toast at breakfast. The salty air, the joyous rain touching my face, the country roads and the accent like the accent here, like that of Grandmother, something gruff. Mother, forgive me for not having told you everything. You know I wasn't hiding anything, but sometimes we just don't know. We don't think of everything and we think the time will come. But the hour strikes too quickly and we weren't able to say. Bernadette at Nevers... I wonder if she's still there, if she's still inctact, if she is crumpled, if

time caught up with her, the beggar, your perfect one. I
wonder whether the sisters of the Trinity are still gently
lifting up vomitting girls who have lost their Mother in
the compact crowd of the miraculously cured. I wonder
whether you are as happy as she is. As your entombed
saint who smiles at death. And often it consoles me to
think that in your funereal cradle, you are just like her,
that death is sweet for you and suits you so well, that
death is salmon, tinged with pink, and that you don it
and decorate yourself with it. Maybe it's wrong to see
you in tatters, like meat and morcellated. Perhaps you
are whole and safe, immaculate. Perhaps your daughter
the doctor is foolish to calculate thus, scientifically, the
minutes of your putrefaction. Maybe I have everything
wrong and God exists, and God has good reason to
laugh at us. Maybe in paradise, Mother, you are beatific,
you watch over me and over my child. Just recently,
Rose saw you in a dream. With all the pills, I have
trouble dreaming. Nothing appears to me anymore.
I'm a positivist, but it's stupid to think one knows that
the dead have fallen silent. Bernadette, your friend, my
God, how I hate her, my God, how I wanted to prove
to you that she was nothing but bullshit. I was wrong,
of course. It's important, all of it. Happiness is in death,
the place of our burial. We spoke immediately, at the
very start, of corpses and tombs, me and that man I
loved, because it seems I did love him, Mother, and not

95

just you. You know it well, in fact, you were happy for me. You didn't want to tell me how much you hated him, but you told him, you threated him with revenge, your own, and that of your saint, the dead warrior. She's not an easy saint. She's not to be trifled with. You were afraid, Mother, you trembled with horror just as one day I cried in secret for my Rose. For my beloved daughter who will embrace horror one day, who's going to bite the dust. And what can I do, if not ask you in your magical beyond to eradicate evil and make good grow? I will do like you, I'll pray to your saint and I'll hide my vivid worries from Rose. I imagined my death with that man, you know. I saw myself lying at his side for eternity. Now, now, I can hardly look at him for more than a second without the mad desire to disfigure him. I find he smells bad, he smells of badly cooked lies, and I hope he'll suffer in hell. Would that it exists! But he won't pay. There is no judgement. Life perpetuates itself, like a perfect crime. Bernadette wanted to do good. You would compare her to me when you would tell me, Mother, that I was a missionary. I would have wanted, like her, to give myself intact, to submit myself without any doubts to the calling. But I vomitted outside, as soon as I went out. The glass shrine made me dizzy. I could have been a saint if I had had faith, if I had believed in God or something like that. I wouldn't have fallen into the clutches of the ogre who served me love, who gave me the impression that life was tender. Better to be a saint and adore only God. Better to be exposed under glass in a vacuum. Better to pray during the day and sleep at night than to love a man who will tear you to shreds.

Mother, I think I have loved before. And I do mean love. But I think it was you and your sleeping saint. I think I only ever loved you, because it was death I was after, smiling death, the death that takes us, death in the company of a being or a creature, the death that awaits us with a God beyond. Mother, I think that in love, I have only ever known you and Bernadette. An intact love, scored by nothing, a lacerating love.

Mother, there was only you, and now there is Rose. I will take care of life. But not like before. You mustn't hold it against me. It seems I have loved before and I still love you. But you're not here anymore... And neither is he, in fact. So I am liquidating you. I am erasing you. I will only love the living, I will only cherish the loving. God forgive me for betraying you or may a gigantic inferno expiate my life.

Five

THIRTY YEARS AFTER he left, here comes my brother.
He's changed a lot, but he's still intact. A mean monster,
a war amputee. He keeps saying the Jerries won't get
him. Born in 1951, he never experienced any of that.
But he likes to complain and is always demanding
compensation and reparations. He says he had a hard
time of it, that Germans are dirty. He gibbers on mixing
the French language soup with the very Germanic stew.
Passed through this mixer, his language isn't recognizable
anymore. It's a stinking spread. Of course I'm not asking
for seconds. But the Crackpot carries on. He unpacks
his salad. He pushes me to the edge, he does it on
purpose. I get stuck with Germania, the Rhenish battles,
the Luftwhatsit, the Nazis like dogs, the pain of war and
the gas that kills. *Achtung!* And he snickers endlessly as
he tells me everything. Florent is a great amputee, like
my grandfather Ferdinand who died in a bombing. *The
Second World War* doesn't sound the same to everyone.
Sometimes it's like a knell or else like recall. Grandfather
Ferdinand died a long time before my birth, but I know
him better than my grandmother Flora whom I seldom
saw and whose name I inherited. I didn't want the a.
I didn't like it. Go figure. I even changed my name.

It needed amputating, a prosthesis for that stemless flower. So I added the *e* and now I run like a rabbit. The operation went well. Better than Ferdinand's. He had his leg cut off in 1917 in Switzerland. My brother lives through that story. In the end, when my mother lost her left breast, after losing the right one, it was definitely on our minds. About ghostly papi's missing leg, the papi I didn't know, but whose prosthesis drags its feet and makes such a rackett in my dreams and nightmares. It's crazy how Ferdine is so present in my life. I wonder what he's doing there and what the Crackpot thinks he's doing by thinking he's him, the 20th century, the world wars, hating Germans and hobbling along on rainy days. I'm sick of that animal's limp. I can't take him stumbling over the slightest pebble and making himself into a maverick at the slightest skirmish. Why play over the destiny that's already having one over on us? I knew Flora. She wasn't very nice. A dreary Norman who counted all her money. She died a syphillitic, well after her husband. It was his heritage, a good heritage he'd brought back from his rounds at Vire, in one of the brothels of the day. I couldn't stand Flora. A drab peasant. She only ever gave me one gift. My communion watch. I don't know what I've since done with it. She must have lifted anchor.

I've got to extract myself from the past, get out of my ancestral stranglehold. I went to my grandparents'

grave in Amers-Bocage. It's no great thing. I have a hard
time understanding how Mother wouldn't have hated
being buried there. Eight years ago, I visited the beaches
of Normandy, the graveyards by the sea and even the
German ones. And then I found myself at Amers, Flora
and Ferdinand Hubert's village. I thought of the women
denounced by Flora. Of the women who slept with
Germans and of the church square, one morning after
the war. That's where they were shaved. I mean:
amputated... Those who got off with some bad German,
my grandmother took care of them. With her, there was
no fooling around. *The war is awfully bunched up and
Flora isn't tender.* I understand why my mother, Violette,
left the maternal soil and wanted to blossom elsewhere
with her husbands. All the beautiful Québécois. And I
think they look alike. My mother's four sisters all
unpotted themselves to graft onto liberating soldiers.
They married good and sane Englishmen, Americans
and Canadians... For that, it's worth redoing all of
D-Day. Only my mother came to Québec. She replanted
herself in the land of deserters, draft-dodgers. I think she
did it on purpose. But grandmother made neither head
nor tail of it. A Canadian remains a Canadian. And that
soil only grows the best flowers. Flora the enthusiastic
became disillusioned after a winter at La Malbaie, with
Papa. Flowers don't grow too well in frozen soil, and the
river only transports violet ice. She wasn't very amused.

She quickly returned to her village where she planted several green vegetables and milked her cow to the last. She died milking. A staggering heart attack. They found her stiff among the daisies. Rosalie, impassive, was grazing as usual. Flora never bought anything. She was a true Norman. My watch, and that's all. Never a little gift. My aunt Marguerite, the youngest of the daughters, confided in me that she often thought of killing her mother, Flora. It's true that she stayed with her mother until the age of thirty-five, until one of the sisters, Muguette, the eldest, who took off with an American G.I. in 1945, found her another American, just as smooth-talking, who liberated her from the infernal maternal clutch. Marguerite had wanted to push Flora down the stairs into the cellar on the sly, if you can believe it. Boom-badaboom... What an accident! I don't know what stopped her. She was sick of eating potatoes to save some money and have even more of a feast when my uncle Narcissus visited Sunday at noon. He was beautiful Flora's only son. He died very young and my God did she mourn him. Her five daughters having taken off in airplanes, very, very far away, hardly phased her. But having her son in Rouen, and then finally in Paris, that made her suffer. She saved it all for him, for that big vegetable who died at the wheel of his blue Mercedes. Because the Germans are still the best when it comes to fast cars. And it's true that that car was a fast

ride. In fact, he died by it. I never really knew him. And
my mother didn't like him. A strange clown. Buried in
Paris. He wasn't interested in his cloddish origins,
flowering beds, fields as far as the eye can see, harvested
wheat and enemy Germans. He wasn't interested in his
parents' past. He frequented a Parisian woman whom he
killed in the accident. They both died instantly. At any
rate that's what Flora told me. But I prefer Marguerite's
story and her desire to liquidate her mother in the cellar
stairwell. I often tried to talk about it with Mother, the
tragic end Flora escaped by the skin of her teeth. But
Violette didn't believe me. *Marguerite is exaggerating.*
She's the spoiled one of the litter. She's lying to make herself
interesting. That's what my mother said. Maybe she was
right. But me, I dreamed of having a stairwell to knock
Flora down, when she came to America to visit her
daughters and marvel at everything. So I visited her
grave eight years ago, and I could see that the Crackpot
had been through shortly before me. He'd left a note for
my grandparents. A note in plastic, a really macabre
thing in which he promised to avenge them in Germany.
I always thought that's where he spent the last thirty
years. I couldn't confirm it, but my little finger tells me
that that's what must have exerted such a strong draw on
him. He must have been living in Frankfurt or
Düsseldorf or even in a hole full of little Nazis. He
couldn't help but relive it all. Me, I couldn't leave

Violette. Only my brothers imagined themselves elsewhere. Genêt in Paris, Florent in Germania or else in Austria, in a sordid village in Rhenania or in Irgendwo. I don't know. My grandfather was born in 1889, like Hitler, several days apart. Adolf, April 20th, and Ferdinand, May 12th. They died the same year. The coincidences of history are ironic. It makes you wonder if you think about it too hard, when you put two and two together and look up close. It all gnawed at my brother's brain. Inside of him there was a big hole, a big amputation. He became Ferdinand, or some French guy, born in 1889. And when he shouts: *dirty Jerries,* he's simply repeating our grandfather's words. In Amers, the gossip spoke to me of my grandmother. It's not a good memory. She wasn't easy. She had a tobacconist's shop and supplied the whole region. Even during the war. But not so much the Germans. The whole region died under a shell or a cancer that Flora passed on for the nation. She killed the whole country. For miles around, she did her work, flogging tobacco. She didn't smoke and none of her children wanted to touch cigarettes afterwards. It's the smell of childhood, Mother explained to me. All that tobacco simply smells bad. Mother died of a fulgurating cancer. Smokes or no smokes, our cells are weak. The Germans of the district returned all fresh to a Germany in ruins that was asking for life. Of course, many fell like flies during the landings. In Normandy, the shells were hitting, and let's face it, they were hitting hard. They were coming down in droves. The Germans were being deducted. And Flora and her kids took to their heels. Exodus... She'd wrapped the stash around her middle. Flora was far-sighted. All the money was there. Her husband was going to meet up with them. He was coming, he was coming. *Go, go now, I'll meet you pronto.* He had to say goodbye to a girlfriend in the city. He caught an American shell full in the face, never caught up with them, but Flora carried on. Her children at her heels, and with the encouragement of her neighbours, Flora's exodus was to flee the Allied forces. She got out of there fast with the Jerry soldiers. Bombs were going off like fireworks. Magnificent flowers in the Norman sky. And a clear hole in the place of the house. That's what was left after the landings. We have very few photos of the whole family. Several Parisian aunts must have filled in the gaps. In the fifties they sent along what they'd received in the mail during the twenties. *But it's all in my head, said Flora. I remember everything.* That particular defect must be hereditary or else it's tied to the floral name. Even with having removed the a, memory doesn't go away. That memory persecutes me and besieges the Crackpot who can't recover from it. With him, it's always, everywhere, Nuremberg. Laments against God, Himmler and Goebbels. He declines hatred in the present, the past. There is no future. Here is Flora, here is Ferdinand. He speaks to me of the BBC, but not the BBC of today, and awaits the 18th of June ferociously. I resent him for making the dead speak. I would like for him to bite the dust of those who've bitten him. I feel like shit for wanting to sweep everything aside. For wanting to make the past into a pretty pile dropped into the wastebins of eternity. But I don't want to end up like Flora denouncing the Jerries and their turncoat mistresses. I know they're legion in our country of savages. I know I could spend my life bleating, cursing tomorrow, constantly at war. Yes, because that's what I inherited from Flora, from Ferdinand, a perpetual war. In the trenches, on the front, in the air, on the sea. I'm a parachutist, a gunner, a foot-slogger, or I'm driving a tank through Europe. I don't ever stop. 14-18, 39-45, and then some. Here I am at war again. Against whom? Against what? Against the ennemies. They're advancing in ranks. How well prepared they are. They'll make minced meat of me, but I'll never surrender. At least that's what I thought before Mother died. But here I am giving in, laying down arms. Let the battles end! I ask for peace, the great armistice. When the Crackpot shouts himself hoarse everyday against the Jerries, when blithely he sings a Bavarian air until he loses his voice, me, I wave the white flag and I ask for mercy. I'm sick of the war, I just want to live, to have my *trou normand*. Digest it all and start again. It's

another feast, meals I've never heard of. Let the
Crackpot take on the entire history of France, of Nazi
Germany, of Ferdinand, of Flora. Let him take it right in
the face, let him cut off a leg and send it by registered
mail to the German embassy. He swears he'll do it. Well,
let him! So I don't have to hear it about it ever again. So
I can bury the dead once more. So the landings can stop
landing in my head. Soon they'll all have croaked, those
who were there. How much must we destroy so that it
won't grow back, so that it won't ever bloom again in my
brother's mind, these morbid ideas, these second-hand
executions? *And you're forgetting seventy, eighteen hundred,*
he throws at me when I tell him it's finished, for good
this time. *They've reunited, you don't know what they're*
saying. You're not afraid of war. Are you afraid of nothing? I
plop my delirious brother down in front of the TV, I
show him the wars of the world. *We're in a new*
millenium. Wouldn't you prefer a more contemporary
delirium? I swear there's enough going on right now right
where we are. No need to unearth the dead full of maggots.
Masticate a bit of the present instead of vomiting the past.
Go nuts like everyone else, go nuts in the present. No one
will notice that you're touched. Join the army, go to
Afghanistan. Turn the crank. And forget your Hitler. Now
we do even better. The present is the only real thing. I'm
sick of war. I don't know which one we're fighting
anymore, but I know I can't take it. Will we ever have

peace and our liberation? Ferdinand's sister, old aunt
Suzanne, turned my childhood into a vast battlefield,
even if I hardly knew her. I know by heart all the
departures of those we won't see again, men of the
family decimated in combat. One morning, during the
war, she wanted to accompany her own son, François, to
the train. Before leaving, she entreated him to have a
good and copious breakfast. *The last one before your next
leave,* she added to convince him. *I don't want to force
you, my little one, but do it for your mother. Give her a way
to make herself useful. I make your black coffee, you
swallow several croissants with your father's preserves,
preserves from the Blois, and then off to the station. You
won't be late, I promise.* They did as she said. He ate
everything up, drank two coffees and they jumped into
the car, heading for the Gare de l'Est. He caught up with
his contingent. He seemed relieved, almost happy to see
his mates. *You understand,* my aunt told me, *at twenty,
you have fun with your friends. François was happy. A
happy nature.* He never came back. Was made a prisoner.
Was held for several months in a wretched prison with
several young officers like him. Several days before the
Liberation, they came to get him in his cell. They placed
twenty young men of twenty in the courtyard and fired,
with no trial other than that. Ready. Aim. Fire. Wham!
There's the banger. The war was coming to a close. The
Germans were losing on every front. The Reich was in a

bad way. A real collapse. Those young men had to be put
to death. It was necessary to win; at least on that front.
Look after the pennies and the pounds will look after
themselves! I hear the execution squad has good aim. It's
not so hard to fire in the early morning at twenty-year
old children so as not to lose face. You've got to act like
you're in charge. Be Attila. *After us, nothing more will
grow.* That's how François died. By a small act of
insanity. A last-minute savagery. The rage of the losers.
Something you could call honour. I don't know
François. He died well before my birth. His mother was
still mourning him in the 80s. She compared him to my
brother Florent who'd already taken off without sending
word. Florent looks like François. I think my poor
brother reminded my mother's family, the Hubert side,
of all the sons, brothers or fathers who died in the two
wars. He considers himself to be more like Ferdinand.
Still, all those young deaths clung a destiny to him. Not
easy to live with. Existence takes a real beating. Vroom,
vroom, it's flattened. Life's not coquettish. It's half-
baked. You can't take off like that. There's no way to
adjust your aim. A fine kettle of fish you're in, and all
because of genetics, a few poorly mixed chromosomes
and secret flaws. The Crackpot thinks he's Ferdinand.
He limps like him proudly lugging his gammy leg.

    After having lost her son, Suzanne watched her
brother die. She loved Ferdinand. To prove it, she

exhibited my grandfather's two prosthetics that she kept
in the maid's room. Flora, Ferdinand's wife, didn't want
the artificial legs, but Suzanne rushed to inherit those
war trophies. She'd wanted to share them with her sister
Hélène, who told her to keep everything and hit her up
for a few francs. Hélène was an alcoholic and needed the
cash. Suzanne was rich and accumulated prosthetics.
Her house was a Franco-German museum, a monument
to the dead. And at each of my visits, she would go get
the false legs and parade them near the fireplace. She
asked me to touch them, to see the objects with which
my grandfather had spent his life. And during all that
time, she caressed the wooden leg and the plastic one
ecstatically. Aunt Suzanne was an absolutely singular
person who came from a very poor background. She and
her eleven brothers and sisters had eaten their share of
mad cow in their Norman hole. In 1920, just after the
war that had cost her brother Ferdinand a leg, she made
up her mind, went up to Paris and took a husband. As
good a man as ever, who gave her sons, but was so old
that one still wonders whose children they were. Mind
you, nature isn't quite so fussy. She gives force where it
smells of death and makes a few miracles. But aunt
Suzanne had nonetheless married Hector Louis for his
money and his advanced age. She hadn't wanted to live
with a husband for long and dreamed of coming out of
her destitution. That woman quickly learned good

manners. She often recounted how she had to go about
it. But she was right. She quickly became a bourgeois, at
the same height as Hector who, at a very young age, had
a horseshoe up his ass and etiquette to spare. In fact
Suzanne gave me my great uncle Hector's silver rattle; I
didn't know him but I wear the toy around my neck.
Suzanne liked relics. In a way, her husband was one. And
her three sons as well. Because they died before her.
Michel of a cancer that struck him down at forty, and
Pierre of AIDS, but Suzanne didn't call it that. She said
something else. The fact is she died at ninety-eight. By
that age, it's true there's a good chance you've buried
everyone. Still, she didn't have much luck. And her
living room was always, for me, a cross between a
funerary salon and Ali Baba's cave. The Parisian havoc
where I would go to unearth some piece of the war.
Suzanne was loquacious, she recounted the past. And
her voice will haunt my life until the end. People don't
speak like her anymore, and haven't for some time. One
day that my TV was on without my paying attention to
it, I heard Aunt Suzanne. It was the actor, Jean Marais.
That voice from another era, but that had aged well,
signalled something I couldn't name. The France of both
wars, Paris besieged. A gruff warmth, an intonation
driven by speed that stops suddenly, rests upon a word
to display its sense. A voice made of rhythms and the
depths of a throat cleared in the morning to make the air

vibrate. A theatrical voice of the public square that declaims life like a tragedean. Berma's voice, tipsy Proust might say. A stentorian voice for a woman with breath enough. If I'm old one day, I'd like to have that voice. For the France of the war to inhabit me thus, like a clarion, like a victory, like perfectly controlled breathing! For France not only to be a terrible spectre that vanishes just as I think I've put my hand on it! I want *la vieille France,* rancid France, France gone rotten in the rhythm of my sentences, in that proud way of showing that language expectorates, expels itself, shows itself to the light of day. Nothing spoken softly, everything for the agora. I want my voice grandiloquent, a voice that takes straight off and before you know it makes you an orator, a Prime Minister. I'm sick of my shameful, clumsy tongue, my tongue of secrets and overly well hidden loves. I like peroration, overture, great speeches, prosopopeia and all the epics. In spite of myself, I still like victorious heroes, triumphant battles and the very grave stanzas that bespeak honour. I'm just a surgeon, I sew, I sew pieces back, but I like a language that bellows because it knows what it's saying. And that's what Suzanne was. I listen to her in me capsizing time and I wave at her so that she'll inhabit me even more. And yet she wasn't always very easy. She directed her own like a little boss. After her marriage to Hector Louis, she had her sisters come to Paris. Each younger than Suzanne, they were all of age to find a rider and marry. Suzanne educated them. For over a year, she showed them what she herself had learned on the fly, by gleaning, copying. She made young ladies of them and married them off. Hector knew all the elite. And in her apartment of the rue de Rome, Suzanne invited, introduced and engaged all her people. Her sisters owed it all to her. In Deauville, the beauties were put on display on the stages of the snobs. Men turned around, they were dazzled. That was the goal, to raise the bidding, and it was achieved with success. Suzanne took advantage of this infinite debt to submit her sisters in order to obtain favours from them, but also to ensure infinite recognition. Hélène was the only truly ungrateful one. She had married the son of a French field marshal, a marshal from the war of 1870. Lucien, the son of a large, good family, was destined to medicine, but never worked since during his studies he fainted at the sight of blood. Medicine was certainly not his cup of tea. His parents were rich, he was an only son. The old died young. And Lucien was heir. Hélène as well, of course. Life changed then. Until then, it had been necessary to comply with mother-in-law, with father-in-law, with Suzanne's dictates, to have good manners, not cross one's legs. But once the in-laws were buried in Trouville in a private cemetery facing the sea, Hélène introduced her husband to the beautiful bohemian life, voyages galore and alcohol in streams. He

113

wanted nothing more than to learn how to slum it. It's what had pleased him so much in this pretty young girl, her naughty air, the air of shamelessness in this girl who's best not messed with. They settled in Normandy on mother- and father-in-law's property, not too far from the cemetery, and had fun at the casino every day. It lasted forty years, forty years of mad passion. They lost, they won. They needed the bicycle to go and gamble daily. Lucien ended up dying and Hélène buried him. Those two had no children. *Too egotistical, too in love, too smitten to weigh themselves down with kids,* Suzanne told me, bitter, scornful. She resented her sister for having mixed nuptials with pleasure. *A sexual marriage, that's all we needed...* The other sisters had all understood that duty is conjugal and marriage boring, that it was a job for the poverty-stricken they had been, guttersnipes, hicks like them. But Hélène didn't see it that way. She loved her husband. It does happen sometimes and even in good families. She drowned herself in wild alcoholism. The only thing that saved her for ten years was the bicycle and the twelve kilometres that separated her from the casino. Hélène played every day, just as she had done for so many years with her beloved husband. *I'm going out with Lucien,* she would say to the startled maid taking her hat. *I'm taking him for a ride. He always comes with me.* One day, in 1980, she had an accident. Nothing terribly serious, in fact, but one broken leg.

And at that age, one doesn't recover so quickly. Suzanne rushed to her sister's bedside. My old aunt detested Normandy which she had managed to escape, but she made an effort, she moved in for a time with her sister, the ingrate, to show her how dependent she was on her. Suzanne wanted to extract a thank-you from Hélène, put her back in check. She prevented her sister from drinking and confiscated her bicycle. *You broke your paw, you're not going to start up again. Are you mad, girl? You've passed the age of such folly.* Hélène, in an enforced rehabilitation program, deprived of her outings with Lucien, let herself die. And very quickly. She called my mother and told her that Suzanne was going to kill her. Violette hadn't believed her. She was wrong, of course. In two months it was done. Hélène passed on with her sister by her side preventing her from drinking the calvados of peasants. Hélène wanted to be buried with her husband, in the cemetery connected to the casino. In her testament, she had asked to rest for eternity beneath her husband's coffin. It was necessary to unearth the latter, inter Hélène's white coffin and put the field marshal's son back on top. Suzanne groused. *Hélène is full of caprices,* but she carried out her sister's last wishes. Which increased Hélène's debt. One day, in the beyond, she would realize everything her older sister had done for her. And when Suzanne and Hélène would meet in God's heaven, they would have much to argue over.

Hélène would then end up apologizing one day. She would understand. Suzanne couldn't imagine that in heaven, her sister was waiting to tell her off, to accuse her of assassination, of premeditated murder. In the last years of her life, Suzanne, very very old, confided to my mother that Hélène often prevented her from sleeping at night, that she appeared in her dreams to convey unpleasantries in such a way as to prevent Suzanne from going back to sleep. *And with that, not even a thank-you,* Suzanne confided wrathfully to my mother. *No gratitude and even now, after all I've done. That girl is a whore, a bloody brazen thing who'd bite the hand that feeds her. And to think I helped her as much as I did and even when she wanted to get rid of her children. I'm the one who drove her to the backstreet abortionist. Lucien passed out just as we were about to enter the operating room. That's what they called that room that was nothing more than the bonesetter, the herbalist's children's room. The room was free in the morning, the children at school, the husband at work. I'm the one who held Hélène's hand, while Lucien was fainting to the side or bleating like a calf. That big ninny never had any courage. He's certainly not his father's son, no way! He and Hélène hadn't wanted children. They loved one another too much. But they were like rabbits, always knocking themselves up. There was nothing doing. She wouldn't listen. But of course, I'm the one who picked up the pieces, who had to roll with the punches when Madame was pregnant. Once or twice, I can understand. We've all been there, but for Hélène it was a regular thing. She was uncannily fertile or else damnably vicious. A woman can prevent such things. You've got to know how to go about it. The husband should take a mistress or go see a prostitute. With intelligence, it's manageable. But Hélène, stubborn as she was, didn't listen to anyone. And she regrets it now, I'm sure of it, wherever she is. And she's going to spend a few years more there… Paradise, my sweet, isn't for just yet. She's a tough girl, even at the end. She left turning her back on me, after an argument, didn't say another word to me, Madame was sulking. After all I did for her! Well, it's awful. Better to take care of oneself. Without me, she would have spent her life with mummy and daddy and would have married a country bumpkin from back home. As for kids, she'd have raised a few, the beggar. A baker's dozen, all she could eat. She was a real laying hen, a fertile Norman field. A country girl who would have stayed put if I hadn't taken matters into my own hands, isn't that so? Well, it's best not to speak of all that, my dear, I'm bothering you with Hélène and my insomnia. How are you, my girl, what have you been up to?* My mother would answer in bits and pieces, speak of her children, but it didn't last. Suzanne unleashed herself once more on Hélène, her brothers, her sisters and their ungratefulness, leaning very heavily on the syllable "grate," making a demonstration of the ignobility of the thing, the sororal vulgarity and unimaginable boorishness of the family. The rambling wouldn't stop. The doddering. The verbal motor senility. I have it all on cassette, days worth of tape. In 1972, an American cousin visiting France decided to film all of yesterday's survivors. He made copies which he distributed to the whole tribe. He went to see several of his uncles and aunts, ninety-year-old ingrates. Suzanne was delighted. The cousin put the camera on a table and let it roll. There are hours worth. Because the roundabout started up again the next day and the next day after that. Life turns, it turns, it doesn't stop turning. The others also agreed. Suzanne's whole family, the stovepipe family, got in on the act. And of course, all they talked about were the wars. German tanks, shells from the real war, the war of 1914. And then the passage of time and unreliable brothers and sisters who ruined everyone else's life. They end up hating one another. It's a long lament, a real ancient chorus that reaches for the jeremiade, recrimination, whimpering, and all of a sudden exaltation, amusement. Uncle Raymond is the most loquacious. Cousin Frank ferreted him out in his village. The youngest of the brothers sought refuge there after having tried his luck in Paris with his so well-married sisters. But there was nothing to be done. Raymond was a mannerless type who slummed it in Paris, became a merchant or second-hand goods dealer and hung around in bistros, cafés and

all the gambling dens dilapidating his sister's money.
After many long years of this little game, Suzanne
bought him a tiny little Norman farm in which she
hoped he would disappear. Which he did. He was tired
of wandering in the big city. He'd done the rounds of
possibilities. It had taken a fifteen-year-long Parisian
spending spree for him to miss his little country. He
wanted to see his Normandy again, but he played hard
to get so that Suzanne would cough up. So when the
cousin arrived from the United States, Raymond wasn't
at all used to so many antics. His sisters rarely came to
visit, there was only Hélène who came by on Sundays on
her bicycle, when the weather was good. Raymond lived
alone, and truth be told, not unhappily, but there were
seldom people at his door. So he gave his money's worth
to the American cousin. He was unstoppable. *We got
them good, those dirty Jerries, bang, bang! They died in
spates, they died in a volley of bullets. Like rats. War was
nasty, we had a bad time of it, we had our share of dents,
cuffs, nasty turns of fate, but it was also good, it had its
good sides, the world isn't like that anymore. Things are
worse off now. Progress, progress, but bullshit, progress...
Have humans changed? No, and certainly not the Jerries.
They'll start up again, it's common knowledge. You don't
know them, my little man. You didn't rub shoulders with
them. In America, you're far away, and for that, you're
lucky. No, honestly, you have to have lived with them. They*

occupied us, by God, I ate alongside them. Came and ate at
our place. Requisitioned everything. It was enough to scare
you out of your wits. But we'd been through the fire. With
them, we knew the script in advance. The Jerries are gutless
pansies, they have no balls. You saw how they handled the
Jews, if it's true. People tell so many stories, you end up not
believing anyone anymore. Mind you, coming from them, it
wouldn't be much of a surprise. I'm dizzy just thinking
about it. Some of them were nice enough. What can you do,
many of them were kids. But still, they were Jerries, and we
didn't hang about when they told us to give up our radios.
There was only Ferdinand's wife, Flora, stubborn as ever,
who would have none of it and listened to the BBC at home
in quiet. They could have killed her for that. Well, not at
all! They came by every evening to listen with her. She stood
up to them. A proud woman. Still, it was crazy, if they'd
eliminated her, she would have had it coming. When you
have children, you've got to be careful. I wonder what she
was thinking, that one. And our brother Ferdinand, he
didn't breathe a word. He was in love with her, I guess.
Even if he was a randy devil who flirted with all the girls in
the region. It didn't bring him any luck. If you see what I
mean. Catastrophes, I tell you. Death rained down, like
shells. Vast expanses of flames, miles of dead people that
stank of carrion. But we didn't talk about it. We fled the
bombings. Boom, boom, it hits hard, I tell you. Airplaines
that burst out, humming and pissing down on us. Things

that shook us, pierced our eardrums. A deafening sound. A thundering riot. The bombs were set ablaze, the bombs danced in the sky. The Americans, the Canadians, how prepared they were! Nothing like the Germans. Many did like Malbrook. Marlbrook the Prince of Commanders, Is gone to war in Flanders. They lost lives. *And too many to be sure.* For Trinity Feast is over, And has brought no news from Dover, And Easter is pass'd moreover, And Malbrook still delays. *But that's what war is. There's no telling, that's the way it is. You've got to liberate yourself. You've got to make massacres. After Algeria, several years later, you decide whether you want to go or not. Men can hide, be ostriches. Beasts. But during the real war, it takes place over your head. You don't eat for months on end, your stomach tugs at you. You have a desire to kill, and not just the Jerries. We bolstered one another. The soldiers sang La Chanson de Craonne. Nice song, hey? It brings tears to my eyes. If it isn't all a crying shame. And the rich are richer, while the little young ones, the peasants' children are cannon fodder. Better not to think about it anymore. Let me pour you another. One more the Germans won't get... That's what we used to say. Have a quick drink. And don't think about it, my little man. You come from Chicago. I knew a young man from there. A very well-educated guy. I couldn't quite place the accent. Here we know British, but American, nyet. A good guy. A Jew so he said, he wanted to help. I want to help you. He must have died. I had asked him to*

121

come to the village again after the war, or to send us a card from home. Chicago, I hear it's beautiful, but cold too. The wind is tough. Anyway that's what the little Jew told us. And then I saw photos on TV later on. We haven't got that here, but we had the war. So we're behind, architecture-wise. Entire cities destroyed, houses wrecked. It pains one just to think about it. Le Havre, here, Le Havre where my in-laws used to live, completely wrecked. It was desolated. Better off dead, Monsieur, than to see all that. It's not pretty. It's war. Ah! We did have a bad time of it... It wasn't funny. It still gives you cramps or bad dreams, wakes you in the night. It's really sad. It's enough to make you hostile. We can't forget anything. And then life goes on. We make do. We snap back. Some make their lives over. Others can't. They're completely done for. War breaks men much stronger than us. A commotion that crushes the spirit. After, your mind is soft and your heart torn out. You survive, you endure. You've got to hold on. There's got to be a meaning to it all. Life's a hand-to-hand combat. But we drag our feet. Flip...flop. We strike a sad figure. I've got some friends, well, they'd be better off dead. I don't tell you this with a light heart. But I prefer to be honest before posterity. Still there are some beautiful celebrations. Commemorations. I always attend. I dress to the nines, I've still got style. There's some marching, some saluting, we receive a lot of thanks. There's the word heroism, and then bravery, courage. Twaddle, if you ask me. When you've got to go, you've got to go. It's not because we want to. I was too young to decide. Leaving would have been irresponsible. The old are fewer and farther between. Staying wasn't much better. There are the animals who console one's sadness. My cats, my pups keep me company. That's what frightens me, that the war might come back. Because you can't keep the animals. It's not at all easy. But me, I couldn't live without them. I'd rather die. When they put the Germanies back together, I was scared out of my wits. I was afraid for my animals, for Hortense and Clémence. If they pull out the gas again, we'll really be screwed. I can't put masks on my little creatures. I'd rather be slaughtered by those Jerry pigs than to be separated from them. It's tragic, we become attached. And war can destroy everything in no time. The world cracks quickly, I guarantee it. They'd have some nerve to start up again. Nothing surprises me anymore. History always repeats itself. A philosopher told me so. I even think he was German, that guy. You see how they see the world. There's no beauty in it. Is your camera still rolling, little cousin? I wonder where this is taking us, all this technology. They'll kill people differently but the result will be the same. The poor are the ones who cop it. The rich always find a way. And my brother Ferdinand who died stupidly. Hit by a shell. He wasn't with his family. Working... I don't remember. Me, I was in the army, I'd enlisted. I was the youngest. I don't remember the First War. Couldn't be a hero. I was barely born. I wanted to catch up. It worked out pretty well. But at home, what would I have done? I made the right decision. Now it's over. It can start again. I just hope I can save the animals. They're the only ones worth anything. The only faithful ones. Because women... But you didn't come all the way here to listen to my antics, my stories about girls. In Paris, it was really something. We had a good time. Well, you've got to be young.

My brother, the Crackpot, confided to Mother during her agony that he'd spent several weeks in Normandy with Raymond. Apparently those parasites got on well. I think Florent wanted to experience the war in the same way. I come across Raymond's expressions in Florent's gibberish. The same intonation, the same muddled story. It's incomprehensible. Limpet! It means diddly-squat! Lunacy runs in the family. Who knows whether it's innate or acquired. Is it by coming into contact with Raymond that the Crackpot perfected his discourse? I don't know. But for me too, war is an obsession. Everyone talked to me about it. And when I turn on the TV, there's always a program on the world wars or a Nazi film. We're still fantasizing about the German uniform. Surely there's something seductive about it. I wonder what it could be... A hint of power, perverse cruelty. It gives us pleasure, we've got to admit it. Otherwise it wouldn't be on television day and night. We'd be watching something else. There's only my dad and his wife Céline, the orthodontist, to

protect me from the war. Papa hid. He was struggling
against something else. Against Canada. My dad was
always fiercely patriotic. In him, my mother saw her
way to forgetting. Finally, a man who didn't love war. At
any rate, not that one. He preferred the one he would
lead all his life against the federal government. He
preferred sovereign war, the war of independence. With
him, I was often able to forget the Germans. *Who?* he
would say bursting out laughing. *Think of our future.*
You're a Québécoise, be proud to be one. All we have are
French ancestors. The Crackpot's father was like that too.
Rabidly pissed off, a global-refuser, a mad militant. My
brother was swallowed by his mother's history. His father
didn't exist. He hardly knew him. After my brother's
birth, he took off immediately. The disappearing trick.
You don't choose your lineage or your heritage. War was
in fact mine. Florent's pretending. He's not a Hubert,
he's a pure Létourneau. War was my business. And he
stole it from me... War was my madness. He took off
with it. He still managed to leave me several pieces.
Enough to go off my head, to go barmy. My brother's a
braggart. What can I do with him? I leave it all to him.
Let him have it... That's what I tell myself.

Six

DON'T GO THINKING he's really good looking, the bastard, but he was there, last night, exactly when I wanted to have it off with the first guy to come along. Do it with the first one through. Because that's how cunting life, flaccid life, ploughs into you. *Bing, bang, I screw you my sweet...*

That's how life talks to me. But it's what I wanted isn't it? I somnambulize myself, etherealize myself, erase myself in the banality of things, I'm turning into pulp, it's my gamble. I lay the first guy to come along, I go to bars, girlfriends' houses or restaurants and I smile and I desire and I set in motion the big machine of sexual boredom with a series of orgasms. And last night the machine was running purringly, all purpurin.

If he'd had a wife, that poor guy, I'd have launched naughtily into the adventure without a second thought. Life would have been wrapped up in five seconds. I would have been the mistress of a married man, I would have suffered by making myself believe that one day he'd leave his petty life for me. If he'd had a concubine, a little wife to pamper, to sweet talk, I'd have given myself a paltry piece of adultery like anyone else... It's dumb, but it doesn't happen to me very often. I never have something like this to bite into, something worn, something raw... He was quite simply a bachelor and he was already talking to me about children and saying we should travel together. There was something extraordinary in the air. A scorched smell; the mad future, the crazy future... Mother is dead. I want to live from day-to-day and be like everyone else. Get off with him or someone else, and then forget, fall back into the same bullshit, walk in my own footsteps, fall out of the frying pan and into the fire with a smile on my lips.

This guy wasn't even married. Nothing to make a meal out of, not even the cold dish of revenge on life. After having orgasmed a dozen times, I got up, went straight to the kitchen, I swallowed my five rainbow pills and a tall glass of water and I was gone. *Ciao bambino... I'm going to sew up some bodies. No time to draw you a picture. I only go out with married men. Like anyone else. You should have thought of that... All you had to do was have a big wedding, no holds barred, embrace domesticity, hug the bosom of your family and then one day, with your cock between my legs, admit your guilt to me over leaving your crazy wife. It was up to you to prepare your future. Me, I can only stand provident people...*

He's a kind of glue jar, I've got to face up to it, and more like Crazy Glue than Lepage. He's nuts... A pain in the neck. And I have some experience on the subject. My diagnosis is good. At midnight, when I

get back from the hospital, he's already left a bunch of
messages on my answering machine. Messages of love,
full of promises and impossible words. I don't like that.
I mean: his voice on the answering machine. If you
want to talk to me, my cell phone is with me all the
time. I'm a doctor, always ready for an emergency, for a
catastrophe. Always ready to patch together a botched
life, an agonizing battleaxe life. My cell phone isn't for
dogs. And he should leave the answering machine free
for Mother! If she wanted to call from beyond, I know
she'd choose that way. That's what she did when she
was alive, she left me long messages on my answering
machine. She didn't want to disturb me, but she couldn't
wait to tell me her neighbour's latest piece of stupidity
or to read me Genêt's fresh letter. Mother left me long,
long messages that I listened to lovingly at night when
I got back from emergency. I'd barely set foot in the
door than, after having kissed Rose, who'd been asleep
for ages, I took the telephone and set about my life
with Mother's voice for background noise. Her voice
accompanied me as I ate cold leftover pizza from the
fridge and it's her voice that rocked me as I curled up on
the couch in the living room. I almost always fell asleep
to the sound of my mother's voice, and if it wasn't too
late, I'd give her a brief call, just to hear it again. It isn't
because she's dead that I'm going to stop waiting for her
calls. Anyway, not just yet... I know that Mother still

might call me and even from beyond. I know that one night, she'll be there, at the end of the line, not live, I'm not crazy, but pre-recorded, and that she will have left me a long message to explain what's going on over there among the worms and the angels, amid viscous decomposition and the diaphanous heavens. Her call will help me. Fuck death. Who gave my number to that bachelor? Who told him I existed elsewhere than in his dreams? Hervé, most likely. It was at his place that I met the poor bastard last night. I'd gone to pick Rose up, and Hervé had set the table for several guests. I stayed to have a drink, and then Rose wanted to sleep with Anna. Those two, it's plain to see, they adore one another. That guy was there, and built like a tank. A big beefy redhead. Nothing special. Someone you toss into the dustbin with the tissue and the tight condoms. Not a recyclable guy. Everything I need to become normal again, to forget my nightmares for one night, and my dead Mother. So I had another drink with him at a bar, after having given Rose a kiss goodbye. I'm very free, I flirt in front of my daughter. Like anyone else, no? Who cares! Anyway, Rose doesn't always want to be with me. I am so morose sometimes and I make her talk about her grandmother. I'm so scared she'll forget her, that one day she'll only have the memories I'll have given her. No more grandmother of her own in her memory, nothing but stories off the rack, her mother's stories.

Her mother with her memory like an elephant's, her computer memory, the psychotic memory of a machine contaminated by a hypermnesic virus. Her mother with her prefabricated remembrances. I would like so much to learn how to forget, erase everything from my hard drive. I would need to find an illness to devour my grey matter, to nibble on my Mother, to make her disappear from inside my skull. For everything to blur, for there to be nothing left in my head. Just ruins, rafts of thought floating in the waters of the past, but nothing that I could really grab hold of. Nothing to sail on. My skull empty. Nothing.

I can't do it. It's not for lack of will, mind you, but I'm incorrigible. The past still speaks to me. I have medication, very effective things, life inhibitors, the essentials. Those are the necessities, and then I place everything on the analyst's couch, I leave them there, for him, my shrink, on his crimson cushions, I leave him my shitty days as a deposit. I have a face-lift from using the exfoliating scrub of time. I leave everything behind. I flush the waters of life. I'll have to shake him down, my psychiatrist buddy, my oblivion dealer. The cretin hasn't yet understood that he's to block the circuits of my past, ligature my history. I have to let my Rose live. I'm not enough like everyone else yet. I live too much with the dead. The meds, shrinks and all the rest will end up curing me. I work hard. I fuck the first comer. And it isn't always easy.

This guy seemed to be just like anyone else. I
didn't particularly like him. Well, maybe a little bit...
I should have been more wary. I only attract nutcases,
lightning, castrophes and turns of fate. I shouldn't
have agreed. Next time, I'll draw straws, I'll play eeny
meeny miney mo or blind man's buff. I have to stop
exerting even the slightest will, I must accept anything,
anyone, and certainly not make decisions about any
of it. Let myself be transported by the open air of life.
OK, here we go, I'm going for a ride. I'll let myself be
picked up by the first one to come along. But with me,
nothing is accidental. It's all destiny, tragedy. Aeschylus,
Shakespeare, Sophocles, Racine. I'm like Oedipus,
with me everything turns grandiose, sordid. If I fuck
an unknown man at a crossroads, there's no doubt the
guy is my father. Pathos and company and so on and so
forth. But can someone explain to me why everything
makes sense with me, makes a sign, comes together,
makes a destiny? Why must life's mayonnaise take all of
a sudden, when I am trying every which way to make
it curdle? Like everyone else. I've always grovelled in
luxury, sumptuousness, immensity and fatality. Every
fifteen days, she's at my door. *Knock knock knock, girly,
here I am. I've brought you something grand, a rich gift of
the future. Open up, sweetie, open up. You can't seriously
refuse destiny's presents. Knock knock knock cutie-pie, here's*

a crazy brother who plays at being a ghost, after thirty years of absence... Knock knock knock, here's Ferdinand's leg that visits you from time-to-time in the night when you're so afraid... Knock knock knock my pretty, it's true you're dotty, but that too is a gift, a gift from me. It's a form of election... You see, like grace, an offering, an award of presence. Just for you. A splendid bouquet made of the flowers of fate. But of course, you'll have to cough up. It doesn't come for free. You don't get anything for nothing. And fatality needs for us not to forget her. I need you, my sweet angel. Knock knock knock. Little favours from time to time. That you carry the good word to your friends, small gifts of destiny to several of your friends. You're the one through whom everything arrives. Aren't you lucky that I chose you... I always have something to give you. The New Year's gifts of birth, life and death. It's crazy how generous I am, me, fatal fatality. Hey, don't you find me seductive? Knock knock knock, my benumbed one, open the door, I'll show you my legs, my beautiful legs with my seven-league boots that let me run faster than chance. I'll let you touch my crotch, my sweet darling, my naughty little one and you'll soil yourself in the depths of fatum. Of the very beautiful. It isn't black at all, destiny is red, always more red, erubescent, indecent, an obscene pomegranate, a forbidden fruit you've got to keep in your mouth. You often want to vomit, Flore Forget, my beautiful Flore Forget with your lecherous flower, when I shoved my tongue into your trap, you were streaming all

133

*over, it ran along your beautiful nacarat lips, and the more
I kissed the full of your mouth, the more you resisted like a
demented little thing. I got you, my beauty, I raped you a
thousand times, and destiny penetrated you. You can shoot
up with antidepressants, anxiolytics, and the rest of your
shit all you want. You can team up with your friends, the
shrinks or the pharmacologists, all you want. If I want
you, I stop by without a warning, I knock at your door
or on your beautiful brown head. Knock knock knock,
you're there, and you have to answer. I ring at three in
the morning to announce the death of a relative or I tap
your cheek one afternoon to announce the disappearance
of your dog. And then I descend upon you, here I am in
the entranceway to your building with your batty brother
under my arm, you know, the one you hadn't seen in thirty
years and whom you thought was dead... You're being taken
in, Flore Forget, I fuck you, my big girl, and I know you
like it. I'm the only one who can give you such pleasures...
Knock knock knock, and your mother dies in two months
of breast cancer. It's because I'm there for you, I'm there for
the grandeur, for the splendour of fate. I'm the femme fatale
of fatality and your depression, your desire for normality,
I'm the one who saddled you with that, so that you would
exceed yourself, beg for mercy and meet your death. Knock
knock knock and you didn't even say no this time. You've
become accommodating with time, my beauty. We form an
old couple of amaranthine amours, enamoured with jinxes,*

*and also with luck. With us, something's got to give, it's
got to bleed cinnabar, there have to be blows and I'm the
one to deal them. Knock knock knock my love, my Flore,
I'll deflower your banality. You're a tragic girl. The same-
as-everyone isn't within everyone's reach. You know it well,
my sweet. And then I know that I please you, my Flore, I
know you'll always let yourself be seduced by me. I play the
old beauty routine, the big seduction scene, I talk to you of
history, I mutter certain words to you, I tickle your ear with
my baneful accents and quietly I whisper, without quite
letting on, the names of gods and devils, and you fall for
it, Flore Forget, you can't cut yourself off. Knock knock... I
possess you and possess you again. Over and over. See, you
can't resist me. You melt, you liquefy, you charge head down
at the adventure, you start believing in stars, getting excited
over the madness of the world, submitting to all my desires.
I snap my whip, shh, shh, I make it quiver over your head,
titillating you with my big fleshy lips, and here you are
on your knees before me, red fatality. You hear me. Knock
knock knock, here we go on stage, here are the turns of fate,
here's the trepidating march of destiny, here's the dance of the
dead and their hammering feet. And there you are too and
you want to dance a round. Protest as you will, my deplored
Flore, you can say all you want that you assassinated me
after your mother's death, me, your tragic destiny, your fatal
folly, you'll always be mine my weasel. You know it well.
All I have to do is raise my little finger for you to start your*

Baptist life up again, your life as a prophet, your impossible life, the life of a person who only ever gets abracadabra'ed. I open my legs wide, Flore, so you can see where you're going. In me, into fatality.

It's amazing the effect this voice on the machine has on me. Side effects and maybe more... It's crazy, that's a fact... The voice of the hardened bachelor who's been waiting for me all his life. The voice of the Cinderella-man who never found the right shoe for his foot and who fucks me all night and asks for more. Can't he forget me like everyone else? Can't he leave me in peace and not copulate lecherously with fatal fatality? Can't he just have a screw and leave it at that? Forget about Flore Forget. Forget that one exists, wants something better and even worse sometimes. Forget that one isn't in the mood to stop at that and the sky is not even a limit. Best not to think. That's how I see that the medication is really poorly dosed. I said so to the shrink who doesn't even understand what's going on inside my head. Does he want me to crack my skull against a wall until it bleeds carmine, rosid and rubicund? I demand a snoring life, a vacuum cleaner life, a life that picks everything up, that doesn't leave any stains, that powerfully absorbs good, evil, pain and joy. I'll draw up my own prescriptions... I need two or three seeds of hellebore and I'll be done. Mother is dead, to hell with it...

I swallow several sleeping pills. I've got to be able

to nap, lie down stupefied and delete myself. Sleep
like a bell-ringer, sleep like a stump, like a dormouse,
a marmot, a blessed one, a brute, even myself. I want
my body dead, to carry on as an automaton, a puppet
of the quotidian. I sleep really hard, I dive into sleep.
Here I am, deaf darknesses of the nocturnal infinite. I
fall asleep forever to the tune of little pills and tomorrow
morning, I'll be a night-rider. There is no more night.
Just darkness and I'm not just going down in the
mouth, I'm digging in. Good night, my Flore, good
night, my sleeping princess whom no charming prince
will reanimate. No sweet dreams. Perish the thought.
Nothingness is quite enough.

The telephone rings... It's a tragedy, an abject
infamy. I've got to learn not to pick up at the slightest
call. I've got to understand that the ring ring of destiny
are Ulysses' sirens, I must think to buy wax ear plugs
when I'm in France at Easter. I should have had my
eardrums perforated, gone to a rock concert and
blown up my boom box, torn my earholes or better yet
cultivated earwax and planted flowers in it. Violets, of
course, and a few garnet roses. But I'm a doctor, poor
girl, and it's the call of duty to which I'm saying yes. I
have a responsibility to answer. I don't want to answer
but it won't stop ringing. The answering machine
engages and the beast starts up again. It rings and rings
some more. My mouth is pasty. Zaleplon puts you

to sleep but doesn't wake you so fast. There's a sort of in-between. And then one's elocution on waking isn't always clear. There's a lack of coordination, several little effects... Like a terrible need to piss, but that's because of all the water I swallowed with the pills. That's not on the list of undesirable effects, if I remember correctly. I'll have to answer, it won't stop ringing. Rose is asleep next door, she's not the one suffering. It may be Genêt or even the Crackpot who dealt another pugnacious blow to a buddy... Surely it must be a misfortune, a jinx, hard cheese, shite, a mix-up or a death. It's not ringing for nothing. Or else the hospital, a patient is dying, I'll need to sponge them up, hemostasize them straight away and sew them up with white thread. A hospital is dead people, but not always mine. It's other people's patients, their friends, their parents. I can't mourn everyone. I've put up with it. Given how long I've been working... But it's altogether not the beep beep of emergency, not the very professional winking of the medical cell phone. I'll have to answer. Can't cut it off. It's the ring ring of my life, of a phone that's very much mine. Gotta piss, because I know for sure I'll have to act, I just don't know why yet. I must have drunk a lot last night to be tormented like this with cramping in my lower abdomen! I finally make up my mind. I grab the receiver while making a bee-line for the toilet. As I relieve myself, pissing very heavily, I answer, decomposed: *Yes yes, what is it? Dr Forget here!* Someone cracks up, covering the sound of splashing urine. I haven't yet understood that I'm being woken up at 6 a.m. to have the piss taken out of me. Finally it stops. *I didn't know, my All Flore, that you were a doc, I would have bet instead on a career as an interpreter, something to do with languages, something that lets you shoot the shit, something to do with eloquence. Because you can talk, my Flore, and even while we're fucking, you don't stop talking, you must make your patients dizzy, no? You're a shrink, Flore? Me, you see, I'm a cook.*

If I talk too much, it's the effects of my selective serotonin reuptake inhibitors and it may be the result of my bipolarity. My friend the shrink can't quite tell yet. He's looking for the right diagnosis. But... I don't believe it! It's you, the guy from the other night that I got off with? You're calling to talk about your language fantasies, you've been pestering me since yesterday because you're getting off on the idea that I was going to say big dick to you in Chinese? I'm a surgeon, asshole, languages, mucosa and outgrowths, I sew them up. There's nothing to get excited about, nothing to get hard over. I'm an emergency room surgeon, every day I get up very early and today, I've go to go, I have a job you know! So I'm going to hang up, very nicely. I don't know your name, Sir, but that you are a cook is of absolutely no interest to me. And since I have to wipe myself, since I just finished pissing, I'm telling you because we've already been somewhat intimate together, I say goodbye to you, and be

139

sure not to call back. I only wanted to fuck...

The guy doesn't listen to a thing, here he is starting up again. I hang up on him, but it doesn't stop ringing. Furious, I answer. I'm going to explain to him that I really want to rip his eyes out and his balls. And I know what I'm talking about, I'm a surgeon, I've done it before. I proffer several threats to that idiot, but here he is inviting me to dinner at his place the next day, promising me it will be delicious and that, if I want, I can bring along some pieces of human bodies for him to prepare for me. *A feast, my Flore, nothing's too good for you.* He tells me we have to see one another again, that he needs me. Just a bit. Just once. And that I owe him that at least. He gives me his address. It's not difficult, it's next door to the restaurant. And his name is Vincent, Vincent Rieux. That his name is a laugh, that his name is happy. I tell him I won't take note of it, that I won't come. He'll wait for me tomorrow at 7 and all night long, he'll wait for me the next day and for all eternity. Here is his address again. Do I have something to write it down? I'm the kind who remembers, I'm the kind who remembers side effects by heart, who retains phone numbers thrown to the wind and the names of people in obituaries. I'm the kind of person who remembers everything, who keeps count, who seeks revenge post-haste. But in his case, I'll forget. Memory, we'll eat it with the brains of a silk-weaver or a cheese head. He

comes from Carcassonne, speaks to me of my breasts
like apples and is salivating at the thought of them. And
I'm not to worry, he doesn't even have an ex or else it's
been so long no one remembers. I hang up laughing. He
knows I'm there.

I spend the day at the banquet. Among sick bodies,
bodies I lance and disembowel, I see flesh, a feast, and
among the entrails of an accident victim, a traffic cut-up,
I catch a glimpse of the spread life is preparing for me...
what a bitch. I also see my friend the shrink to have the
dose of my pharmaceutical rainbow corrected, to have
my brain balanced.

I'm decidedly unprepared to eat of that bread, the
bread of happiness. The best doctor is the cauldron, it's
true, but who said I wanted to be cured of life? Who
said I needed a detox? I'd like a few more injections
of despair, of quiet misfortune. But today the grub is
grabbing my senses. I'd damn myself for blood sausage
with apples, omelette de la chanoinesse or even a
charlotte, only moderately Russian. I'm hallucinating
fumet, fantasies, aroma and juice. I can't stop thinking
about it and at night I imagine kitchens filled with
cauldrons in which my fucking existence resonates...
Careful. Jangling ovens, symphonies of knives, spoons,
song of copper instruments, megalomaniacal saucepans
of the future. Of course the medications have effects.
For thirty-six hours I'm in a fairy tale. That of the young

cook who kills himself the one night he botched the queen's dish. That of the genius chef who regales the country. I don't really think of him, the redheaded lover, the lover I won't make a meal out of. I'm not looking to find out who he is, nor what series of moves he'll make. But I see the toast I could make to life, the glasses I could empty while toasting the future, the meals I'll devour, avid to bite into the world.

And all I can do is see him again.

The meals he wouldn't make, the sauces he wouldn't invent for me were already a source of suffering. Before my astounded eyes, at night, on a big festive table, the growing stack of dishes he wouldn't prepare, all the sensuality which, because of my stubbornness, I would be robbed of. I can't mourn what I don't know, what hasn't been. The flesh of the coming world. I can't forget the magnificent, voluptuous food I won't touch, which won't ever play perversely with my palate. I think of all those ghost dishes I'll abandon with my refusal. I like those whose work is immediate, ephemeral. I like evanescent pleasures, pleasures of which there remain nothing more than memories, than the divine taste of what cannot last. I love theatre actors, live dancers, singers, florists. I like artists of the here and now, and suddenness in the act, the immediate lightning of genius... As a surgeon I'm familiar with botched dishes and successful dishes, mayonnaise that takes

or that snaps in one's fingers, that collapses agonizing
at the bottoms of bowls and that I rescue at the last
moment, soufflés that crumple and swell with hope. I'm
familiar with the happiness of the blonde redhead who's
becoming attached, because I know how to wear him
out. I'm familiar with life, real red meat that sweats and
that I fry in a pan. I fix, I prepare meals that must always
be eaten hot. I've got to bridle bodies right away. It's
right away that I'll put on the stuffing of the living, that
I'll smother death in a good pullet sauce.

Shrinks aren't anything like me. Madeleine Lévesque
is a good example. It's really a scummy job. Psychiatrists
don't have quick pleasures, swift gratification. Their
patients only savour the meals prepared for them very
slowly. The zany brains, the broken hearts of the world
don't revel in this way, they don't fall asleep digesting
happiness, burping with ease. Me, I'm jubilant when I
know that life is catching on, the heart is good and in
a month I'll be laughing madly with my disemboweled
patient of the day, I'll be caressing his seam. I savour my
art that struggles against death. In spite of myself.

So tonight I dream of cooks who own fast-food
chains on Saint-Laurent, who fry steaks in a pan to
feed the neighbourhood children and prepare big serial
killer smoked meats, to knock me for a loop. I dream
of men with drippy omelettes who promise me they'll
live forever, to put an end to what is good and dead

and buried. I dream of someone whose entire happiness resides in the pleasure of feeding others, in the pleasure of seeing them take pleasure in life in the present. I dream of a happy cook. Of a redheaded maître d'hôtel with truffled feet who will make me old wives' pig's feet.

And I see him. Here I am, already at his place, in the apartment stuck on top of his restaurant. In his baroque apartment that's making eyes at the kitchens. And me of course. He's there. His name is Vincent and I want to laugh. He's really sturdy and vaguely redheaded, like caramelized sugar, slightly fried butter. Something tasty, even better laid out. Something of a spread. The furniture is alchermes, scarlet, ruby. Something sumptuous. He knows how to live, it goes without saying, and I do not. The French like him, greedy for faith and for me, are just like my Mother and I have the jitters. I'm not seriously going to fall in love with my mother again am I? In his mouth, it's good for the tongue to meander elaborately and then to wander between two mouthfuls of languorous kidneys and offal. This guy gives glimpses of the maternal gesture. Grub, home, ease of speaking, the eyes of a Norman cow slaughtered in Lyon, in a great restaurant, and a terrible accent that cuts like a knife before reaching for another slice. I like his tongue. I like it when he speaks to me and tells me silly words I don't listen to. This man is a brute, a bull, a heifer, and I'm his calf that he

licks passionately, his mouth already full of extravagant
victuals. He's a tough guy with cow's eyes, a gentle,
sad and slightly moist look. And this time, despite the
proverb, I declare loud and clear that only big bulls can
carry out great labour. And how well he works, how
well he works me over, this bull from Carcassonne,
who's come just for me from his ganaderia. In him,
Normandy, the northern death-blow. In him, the polar
bear, the viking boor, the big Norman wardrobe, runny
camembert, the man with big clogs and unfiled nails.
In him, the austral Aude, a crackling, derailing voice, a
southerly wind, an insolent hidalgo and a Spanish cow.
He's all of France, he's my whole mother. The North,
then the South, my grandfather, my grandmother. The
greasy sausage, from Vire, a strong calvados, my *trou
normand* swallowed between two dishes to activate
stomach and body. He's my cabécou from Rocamadour,
my ham from Bayonne, my goat, my very fruity
chabichou. Now I'm convinced it's Mother who sent
him my way. I gulp him with my eyes, devour him, suck
him between the Basque chicken, tripes Caen-style and
a Mère Poulard omelette. He feeds me, stuffs me. I drink
from his udder. He's a real mum. A mother hen who
lays golden eggs and recovers her chicks. And I'm his
little quail, his tup lamb, his docile yearling. I get up on
my dewclaws. I comb my crest. He makes a mouthful
of me, little chicken casserole. How am I to resist such

145

an animal? My bestial love? My unsatiated desires for cruel calving. I want to bring into the world worlds and universes. Engender chimerae, imaginary beasts. Cut up my dreams to better savour them.

There's no doubt I like him, and then I have him again. With a salad and he tosses me. He's a strange boy, a whacko. Here I am straddling a red stool in the middle of the kitchens, contemplating flying spatulas, spinning whips, cutlasses, jacknives, Laguioles, Opinels, fish knives, vegetable knives, cheese knives, dessert knives, butter and bread knives, deep spoons, ladles, pouches, prodigious place settings, oyster forks, thick Mazagran, pewter goblets, slender flutes, fat cups and stout mugs. Now he's breaking all the sated snifters, flinging them one after another to ward off back luck and the seven years of misfortune. We won't pay for our broken glasses. And they're smashing all over the place, there is nothing left but shards. And our laughter, and glass, and porcelain. *For you, I chip, I put a dent in this sad, ugly life.* It rings, it resonnates, a carillon of plates that have just tumbled from the disturbed shelf, a deafening sound covered by our kisses. *It's all I have, you see, I give it to you. Have a bit more to eat, what can I make for you?* And me, I have you raw, I swallow you, I inhale you. Love simmers, moans, slow cooking, contented. And you, you are the best. An infernal nectar, an exquisite food. I'm afraid of biting into you, of consuming you too quickly

or too often. Of leaving you nothing of yourself, of
making myself sick the next day. But you are chocolate.
And that's all I eat. When I was expecting my Rose, life
was either milk or dark, with small chips of bitter orange
rind. I still have the flavour of those fruits of the earth. I
have another piece, just for the tasty tidbit.

You don't know how good you are for me yet. You
don't yet know about my childhood vomiting, my
morning retching, the spew of living. I couldn't eat a
thing and for years this snotty existence wouldn't pass.
My mother was like you. She gave me beakfuls, chewed
my mouthfuls, made me want to be in the tongue's
hollow. My Mother wanted to regale with the world at
breakfast. For me to savour time, long in the mouth, in
unctuous plenitude. My mother was like you, beautiful
Norman beef, a girl of the fields in which simple
flowers like dandelions grew and out of which fine and
deliciously bitter salads could be made. My mother was
like you. Out of a tiny bit of meat, a pickle lost in the
middle of the fridge, out of nothing, two times nothing,
she could make a feast. You're weirdos. Fairies of the
everyday. With you my days can become banquets.
Mother, I was always in the crooks of your arms, in the
movement of your hips, in your skirt, in your feet and in
your aprons. I made myself light so that you could drag
me along everywhere. I'll be in your hat your mad hatter
of a surgeon who can't cook an egg, but handles human

and inhuman livers, spleens and offal. I'll be in your
crown, in your white calico, magnificent and lordly. I'll
nestle there, belching the delight of your dishes. Give me
another piece of you so that I can swallow you whole.
My mother was like you, and honestly you remind me
of her with your desire to protect the crazy spider, with
her touch of madness, and her little moped with a bee
in her bonnet. Yours you wear high and proud on your
red head, on your equine head with jaws that crush me
and that I can't stop stroking with my eyes wide open.
I wanted to forget the maternal plethora, but you are
my Mother, my marvellous mother, a cascade of fruit
juices and flowers, a pyramid of cream puffs, *une pièce
bien montée*. I wanted to erase the bright excesses of our
Violette, but you are abundance, feast, fireworks in my
throat. And I hold on to the taste of your toes dipped in
ravigote sauce, your bovine hands that I eat with spices,
your hatchling mouth in which I experience a thousand
new flavours, your inexhaustible fountain of champagne
sex at which I'll drink myself drunk. I called you Julien,
Julien the Hospitaller, you, Vincent, the painter of life,
the earthly illuminated, the sublime madman with a
smitten ear, with a torn lobe. A little jewel tucked in
your red hair, Dutch flash fires of an ill-extinguished
blaze. You are my catastrophe, my kidney stones, you are
my stomach aches, and I'll die of you yet, if I don't take
care.

I'm mad about Vincent. A moment took hold of
me and I'm well-stewed, burned to a crisp. And yet,
it's in me, all this blood coming to life, I'm becoming
rare again, underdone, well done. I'm being eaten
alive, without a song or a dance. Vincent is cassoulet
but never sour grapes. From Castelnaudaray to
Oustreham-sur-Mer, he serves me up on a silver tray
from France that belonged to my mother, the one she
raised me on. I never have enough raw root vegetables,
spiritual rutabagas. I'm mad about Vincent. His name
is promising. It's a bouquet of helianthus, a magic
sunflower verging on orange. I remember it well: when
I was a child, with my mother and my brothers, our
neighbours were Protestant Germans who cultivated a
vegatable garden, a sad kitchen garden of washed-out
squash. And it grew heavily on the other side of the
wall. And they were good and round, all those winter
squashes, those fat pumpkins, those squat gourds.
My mother often said of the vegetable garden that it
was a podgy pepo and we laughed readily, go figure.
My mother didn't like Germans at all, and for good
reason... And our neighbours gave as good as they got.
My mother had a magnificent garden, a potty paradise
in which floral enchantments grew. Our neighbours,
contemplating our colourful fantasies from the top of
their fenced-in balcony, decided to become decorative,
to dress their vegetable garden and blossomed

marvellous and very tall sunflowers that erected a natural fence between us and them. My mother called that region Alsace-Lorraine and she laughed. And we, her children, we wanted to offer her a bit of her Alsace and all her Lorraine, so much so that we pulled up the sunflower, at evening or night, and we made bouquets for Mother who was very surprised by our thief's gifts and asked us to be careful not to be caught by the Germans. We pilfered the helianthus but never to excess. A few at a time, enough to please Mother! Vincent is that giant cut flower. This flower offered to Mother by her triumphant children. He's a war trophy, the product of larceny, an exquisite maraud. And I have no right to it, but my mother protects me and simply tells me not to get caught, not to take too much. *Just a taste. Not the whole garden. You're not in paradise yet.*

I spend this first night, the second night in fact, in exalted and laughing love. This first night is a banquet of bodies and desires of the mouth, of extraordinary succulences. My pills are so well assorted to flesh! My pills in hiding remind me that tomorrow, certainly, I'll have to... I water it with love. I can't go back. I can only love. I'm mad about Vincent. It's Saint Vitus' Dance. A fox trot, a cake-walk. Choreic, hysterical, pathological. In a flash, I'd throw out the concerted effort of these months spent building dams against dingos like me. I can't afford to fuck up! I'm mad about Vincent. And

that's the problem. I just want to become normal. Not
in love, to hell with it. I simply can't allow myself life,
the days, the nights without a net and off the cuff. With
me, everything goes rotten. I'll putrefy love. And I don't
want that. And I can't take it anymore. Pain in the body
and a bleeding brain. A body full of bruises and the
gasps of a girl who can't stop the torrential flood of tears.

In the morning when I wake, oh! How much better
I feel. He's there beside me, and he's watching me sleep.
I explain it all to him, swallowing a bit of colour with
my lovingly fresh-squeezed grapefruit juice, some pink
and some green. Another green one and another pink
one. There, my day is set. My patients at the front of
the line and my work cut out for me. I want to forget
Mother, love, and then him. I give it all a turn for
the worse. I'm a real sore. With me, everything ends,
everything gets jumbled and mixed up. I'll end up at the
hospital, and since I'm there already, it will be at the end
of a rope. And I want to be alone. There's my botched
misfortune. It's a deal with me. It will end in Berezina. It
will be collapse, bankruptcy, and tsunami.

He promises me the moon. A trip to Pampluna.
A detox treatment. A familial Carcassonne. *We'll have
children. We'll collect souvenirs. Everything but the kitchen
sink, and happiness especially. What do you say, my Flore?
Listen a bit. I'm going to give you the schpiel. You need it.
I'll butter you up and work my magic on you. Let things*

be. Give life its chance. Let the big wheel of your childhood dreams turn. Pray to your idiotic Saint Bernadette and disown at least three times the modern jester god of your medication. Your mother is dead, OK. But it's not your turn yet. Flore, my tragic one, don't you want to laugh a bit? I'm going to get you some croissants and pains au chocolat, and if you die one day, it will be of pleasure. It will be for having come too hard over everything and even nothing. Over me, the big restaurant and the bed that gives you shelter. Flore, my Flore, introduce me to your daughter and your brother and let's go see your mother at the cemetery tomorrow. I'll ask her for your hand, I'll ask her for your soul, your body, your waste and your tears. I want you, Flore so moist, my flower that I water. I'll nourish your earth, I'll fertilize you and you'll grow back. Let me love you in front and from behind and then on the sides, in all your orifices. Let me penetrate your big heart, it's too big for you alone, I want to settle and dwell there for many long years. Flore, I'm sentimental, it's true, but I won't make you flowers or favours. I'll tell you things that are true, things we don't know. On St. Valentine's Day everything melts, everything caves in, you see. Here, now I'm making you laugh. But let life frolic rather than wilt. You aren't stained or sullied. You are the flower in bloom. My little daisy. You're not a Good Friday. You are the flowering spring or a real Easter Sunday. Eggs and bells. And chocolates. Flore... Chocolate bells I'll have made for you by another Vincent,

my master confectioner. Come on Flore, grapefruit, orange
like me all around your mouth, finish your fruit juice. You'll
call work. You'll say that you're sick. We'll go for a wander.
Along the Saint-Laurent, the river I love so much. It's cold
and it's snowing. But I'll start up the car. It will be good to
laugh and kiss your neck. Flore, let's go. At least one more
round. Or two, or even three.

Seven

IT'S CRAZY HOW we age. It creeps up slowly, a slight
physical defect, a little stain on the hand, a slightly
coarser laugh, and from there it proliferates. We become
a weed, abundant dandelion and crabgrass. The skin gets
flabby. Tubers and outgrowths blossom. The gift basket
of time. Everything topples, slowly we collapse. It was
only a matter of time for me. Just after Mother's death.
I had to follow her in a sense, decompose at the same
rate as her, fall to pieces, let myself go down the drain.
I've fallen a bit behind, it's true, but my eyelid is crow's-
footing, I'm cock-eyed, I'm turning into a buzzard, an
old vulture with gnarled fingers. I'm in love and the
timing is off. I'm too old. There's nothing virginal about
me. I'm forty-five and I look it. So many years and more
that won't come back. So many days and more that
gather beneath my skull and that I dream of forgetting.
That's what's hardest of all: forgetting. Especially when
the past knocks at your door, when your brother shows
up from the ends of the earth, after thirty years, and
your devilled mother has passed on unannounced. "I've
more memories than if I were a thousand years old."
Time has settled into my body, time has coiled into my
life. Out of the blue the bastard dug himself a nest and

honestly, here he is still hoping to make little ones. Best
not to disturb him... There's no place like home! I'd kick
the fucker out if I could. Git! Sweep him clean out of
here! And the Crackpot with him! Out of here in short
shrift and no complaining! I'd clear my mind and have
a big liquidation! Put an end to everything. But in the
meantime, the bastards gain on me. Time is hell-bent.
Happy. Your mother's dead? Good, that's how it is. The
order of the world. The order of time. I can't fight, I'm a
Mother. We're fouling ourselves at practically the same
speed. I console myself thus, by thinking of simultaneity,
synchronicity and the whole shebang. And then there is
my Rose who is beckoning me, who brings meaning to
light. There is my Rose who says: "There are perfumes
cool as children's flesh." Rose is. She will be. And time is
more sweet to me. Time is less furious. Rose is wiggling
there. She parasites time, sucks its sap. I hope it will
croak. And then there is Vincent, the laugher that gives
me facelifts. My skin is tightening again. My ass stands
to attention, erect with joy.

At work, they're all bastards. Pigs I'd gleefully
slaughter, dismember in a flash. I'm a surgeon. I know
how to make someone bleed. They want my hide, of
course. Even my used, weather-worn and war-torn hide.
There isn't much glory in taking it out on mourners, on
girls who've died from grief, on weeping Antigones,
orphans of History... It isn't very pretty to scheme

against intelligence, to assassinate genius. They want to see me disemboweled, livid, at the end of my blood, asking for mercy. They won't sew me back up, won't stop the hemorrhaging. Too much pleasure in seeing someone suffer. And they're the ones who are incompetent. I don't even know if they know what to do. They cover one another, write one another indulgent letters, raise a left hand to bear witness. Blah blah. The soap box of the confraternity. When I think of that bitch of a hospital director, that talentless scalpel wielder, that twat who found her diploma in a Cracker Jack box, who became a psychiatrist because she pleased the anesthestist, a fat Englishman, I want to run each of them along my scalpel. It's the fat Englishman who directed the show for thirty years on the sly. He wanted so much for women to have their place in order to unseat men more intelligent than himself. But there is time, which will sort them out, those rotting interiors, those pathetic puppets, blatant and barefaced. They're ignoble for wanting to make believe they haven't aged, haven't a wrinkle on their faces or asses. At work, they're real squealing sows, the crapulent director and the old anesthetist who promises to retire before going soft in the head. He can control everything, that old fossil, that stuffed, overblown windbag, that revolting man who grew breasts. And they aren't beautiful and they aren't fresh... That guy's probably going to kick it in an

CATHERINE MAVRIKAKIS

operating room. Give up the ghost. And I won't
resuscitate him. I'll let him howl. I'll let him agonize
with his mouth gaping. How many anesthesias did that
incompetent nitrous oxidizer botch! How he made my
work impossible! And that Madeleine, the director,
always protected him. Of course you've got to close
ranks when you're second-rate, show some solidarity.
Madeleine is the President of the Order of Physicians
even though, in the context of her duties, she fires
anyone who refuses to eat from her hands. A real cunt.
But the Lévesque is growing old. She's taking a turn for
the worse, turning like a bad mayonnaise. She's
becoming downright decrepit, with fat jowls, dropsical
rings and bulgy eyes. She still smiles at me when we pass
one another in the hallways, she smiles at me as though
nothing were the matter. As though she weren't building
a dirty case against me, as though she weren't waiting,
pulling her tongue and pulling it hard, for me to
commit the tiniest medical error, just enough to send me
packing, just enough to have me exterminated. I know
her, my Madeleine. We studied together twenty-five
years ago. She already had two diplomas to her credit
and I don't know how many lovers, doctors in their pot-
bellied fifties who wanted to show her the ropes. She
couldn't even get into medical school on the first try. It
made her sick to see me so gifted, to see me pass my
exams, my dissections and stitches with my fingers up

my nose. I know my way around organs and bodies. I've
always had some talent, medical talent. It's not much.
But Madeleine didn't even have that. So she finished her
studies the best she could, mortally jealous of me, all the
while calling me her friend, her great friend. And don't
you know it, she went into psychiatry. Only there could
a lazy person such as herself go, and fast, really fast, she
climbed the ranks. The fat anesthetist, that crawed cock,
was already watching over the barnyard. Madeleine
spent her time at cocktail parties, *5-à-7* and the drinks
to good health of some underling, she rambled in the
Boards of Directors by making pronouncements with
her air of well-informed womanhood. The fat English
anesthetist took him under his big chubby wing and
Madeleine became someone. A shit-disturber, a doer of
little, an entrepreneur of the void, a slut of the worst
kind who worked hard for the cause of Polish doctors
because she wanted to get laid by all of Eastern Europe.
It makes it much easier to close their mouths... For
years, I used her. I made good use of that squiffy,
unkempt drunkard who looked all day long like she'd
just got out of bed, with the stupefied demeanor that she
bandies about. I didn't attack Madeleine frontally. I
made grandiose suggestions and never said a mean word
about her boyfriend, the fat English anesthetist who
directed and continues to direct the hospital by proxy.
All the competent doctors ended up splitting. In my

hospital, there are only clods left, young people or falsely innocent people who want to believe that Madeleine is a great lady, a great psychiatrist, a great committed soul. I didn't want to leave. I decided that life would be a battle. And I was wrong. Now Madeleine wants my hide. Mother is dead. She thinks I haven't been properly paid back. I must be tortured. The fat emasculated Englishman wants my head. It's true I've asked not to have to operate with him anymore. I fear catastrophe. He doesn't even know how to measure out Valium, and with the enflurane, he makes blunder upon blunder. I can do better than he can. The residents aren't fooled. But the fat greasy Englishman is convinced I'm the one calling the shots against him. I've got better things to do, man, than to stack the youngsters against the English! It's been ages since I've wanted to bounce you out of my place. I've got my share of Joan of Arc, but you know people like you are always the stronger. Since Mother's death, I don't think of you anymore... Against the carefree violence of the world, I can do nothing, I raise my arms, shrug my shoulders and think of my meds and ways to get rid of my brother, the Crackpot, to find him a home sweet home, far away from here. I also wonder how to devour my lover as the dish of the day. I don't give a toss about you, my fat Englishman who wreaks of halothane and methoxyflurane, don't give a shit about Madeleine Lévesque and her whole bishopric. But

because I don't have my eye on you anymore, you the fat
decrepit one and the little dimwit, you've decided to
liquidate me. OK, go ahead, split hairs. My doses of
medicinal happiness won't get me fired. You and
Madeleine, you've been stuffing yourselves full of
tranquilizers and getting off on Prozac for so many years
that you don't count anymore. You'll have to find
something that will get me fired, and I won't help you.
I'm here, I'm staying, and I have no desire to find
another crib. If I'd wanted to, I would have left for the
United States twenty years ago, but I'm true to myself
and won't sell my soul to the devil. So the three of us are
going to grow old together, unless the fat sexagenarian
Englishman kicks it from a heart attack in the operating
room when I come in and say Boo! to him; unless
Madeleine swallows too high a dose of barbiturates. She's
been messing around with her prescriptions for a long
time now. But you see, comrades, I think we'll finish
among friends, in a rotten hospital which I won't leave,
because I know that anywhere else is just as foul, in a
Raft-of-the-Medusa-hospital that you can't leave because
no one wants you. We'll perhaps all die together one day
when an exasperated patient will come into the hospital
and gun everyone down. And he won't be in the wrong.
Because that's the perfect irony, or else, life in all of its
meanness, Madeleine, me, and the fat Englishman, are
bound to the end, even if our hatred is fierce, and our

contempt expansive. To grow old, my pretties, happens with whomever. Yep, we'll croak like brave little soldiers at war with death. Yep, we'll die synchronously, because none of us will have had the courage to blow our head off, to throw it all away. That's what growing old is, my old friends, it's not choosing one's death, but knowing the hour and furthermore, the place. It's knowing with whom and also how. Madeleine, do you remember Milena Ayzerstein? The first years, all three of us were friends. A magnificent girl I was in love with. And you too, Madeleine, you loved her in secret, but you just thought you were jealous of her. You always expressed your homosexuality like that, in the mad envy of others and what they had. By stealing their boyfriend. But in this case there was nothing to steal. We loved Milena. And more than anything, I loved the white of her breasts from which I drank during our years in residence. She was authentic. Even more talented than me. A staggering surgeon. A genius of a doctor. She had everything going for her. That's what people say. Well, they're right. And then one day, wham bam, madness and bedlam. Do you remember that awful day when we were on duty together, when she confided to us that she had to go home, see her parents again and her brothers, get married and have children. She owed it to her family, her country, her siblings and life. I resented her for not having told me in secret, for having learned it at the same time as you. But what can you do, Madeleine, I told myself that it was easier for her that way, easier to give an official speech, a speech before an idiot like you, a goose like you. I often used this strategy afterward, to speak the truth, that cost me, and that I wasn't able to say. I often imitated Milena, I copied her in everything. That way I could keep her for myself. In imitated gestures, her drawings of smiles, her accent that I donned at night in tears. I often dropped a volley of sad, hard words to inform those I love of what I couldn't tell them. Milena wasn't stupid, telling me she was going to leave me at the same time as she confided her intentions to both you and me. Your flabbergasted, dim-witted demeanor, fat cow ruminating your impossible revenge and your innate stupidity in some ways cushioned the blow. It's amazing how you helped me at that moment, Madeleine. Milena left shortly therafter. I knew she would leave one day. Milena hadn't hidden anything from me. But I think I also saw her here, with us, for always. I didn't imagine her elsewhere. We learned that she'd married, was the director of a large hospital over there, that she'd had a daughter. I have photos of Marina. I'm her godmother. Yes, that's how it is. Her godmother. We also learned that on the morning of Sunday May 23, 1989, Milena went out to buy cigarettes from the stand some five hundred metres from her house, a little further, on the other side of the tracks.

She bought a pack of Pall Malls, which we used to
smoke together, she and I, when we were on duty or
even in bed, at night, when we were young and crazy.
We certainly were crazy. May 23, 1989, in the morning,
Milena seemed in a hurry. She told her husband she
needed cigarettes. She pulled a coat over her nightgown.
She went to the door of the apartment. Hurriedly. She
stopped dead, thought for a moment, not long, you
know how fast things move, we don't think, we act. She
moved, still very quickly, toward the blue room, her
daughter's bedroom, my goddaughter. Marina was
sleeping. Milena looked at her and kissed her on the
forehead. She ran to the door. She was in a hurry, as
though she were running after something, a train that
was slipping through her fingers. Milena ran to the
smoke stand. That morning, May 23, 1989, her cousin
was there. It was her cousin who sold Milena cigarettes
everyday, at that stand in that little Eastern European
city to which Milena had returned to change things, to
transform life, alter the world. With a tap of her western
wand, with a slice of her North American scalpel. Her
cousin sold Pall Malls. I don't know the detail of the
transaction. Did Milena pay that day? Did she tell her
cousin she'd pay her later, on another day? Did she ask
her to put it on Milena's tab, the doctor who'd come
from so far away? From Canada. To make a new life.
Why not? We learned that Milena hadn't lingered that

day to chat with Livia, her cousin, her childhood sister. *I don't have time, this morning, I'm in a hurry,* answered Milena when Livia asked her to stop for a couple of minutes, to talk about and give her news of Marina, that marvelously blonde child, my goddaughter. Milena took off quickly. She was looking at her watch. And then, no one knows. We know she smoked near the rail line. We imagine it. A cigarette butt was found there. A Pall Mall. Of the pack, nothing remains. We know that the train went by and didn't miss Milena. She died on the spot. That death is a quick death. Not much to be done. I have often had to take care of train wrecks. There's nothing pretty about it. Milena must also have been familiar with that death. She was a surgeon like me. But much more talented than I. At the spot where Milena finally caught the train, on time, right on time, for years, there are crosses there. Many crosses. Five or six, I've been told. Milena couldn't have missed them. Every day she passed in front of them on her way to buy cigarettes. The crosses create a safe place. You can catch the train there. The last train. The crosses attest to the efficacy of the trains, the punctuality of death. There's no doubt that Milena received those very dead at the hospital. She lived in that little city in which the train is still a sign of freedom, a perhaps preferable elsewhere. It's by that train that she returned home years earlier. Against her will. But for her country, her father, her mother, her children to come. *I have to pay my dues,* she often said to me. *You don't know what it's like.* No, I didn't know, Milena, I didn't know anything about your atrocious suffering, your absolute, ravaging despair. I didn't know you'd catch the train that day, Milena. You were so talented, so beautiful, so white, and I was beatific with admiration. At university in 1977, there was you, the most talented doctor at the school. You, the medical genius. You, so human, so intelligent. Everyone believed in your success. In your glory. In awarded prizes, honorary doctorates, honours, decorations, orders of merit and flowers, flowers of every colour. The red carpets of life laid out just for you, Milena. In 1977, at medical school, there was also me, and that bungler Madeleine Lévesque. You see what has become of us. Mother is dead. You too. Me, you see, I'm not doing very well. Despite this love I'm so afraid of spoiling. Like everything else. I'm a good doctor, it's true, and I don't know if I could have done better. Maybe I should have caught the 8 o'clock train like you, one Sunday morning in May... Maybe that's what I should have done, several years ago now. I wouldn't have learned of your death, nor Mother's. I would have known nothing about age, time that passes and mows you down, but not like the train. Not as effectively. I wouldn't have been orphaned of my Mother, a survivor of myself, a very good doctor, sure, but only that: a very good doctor. I really think I should

have caught the train instead of you that morning of
May 23rd, 1989. I wouldn't have had to tell myself that
I'm going to die slowly of a lung cancer, because I smoke
too much, Pall Malls as a matter of fact. I quit the Lucky
Strikes. I don't believe in luck anymore. And I know
how bad it is, I'm a surgeon, I've done hundreds of
partial or total ablations. I'm familiar with both
pneumonectomy and thoracoplasty. I don't see anyone
operating better than I do. Besides, of course, Milena,
but she died in a train caught on the fly, in a train that
carries people to an elsewhere from which they won't
return. Milena's whole family knew the taste of trains.
Her father had escaped by the skin of his teeth. Late for
a meeting, his mother had had to leave the house with
her daughter during the roundup from which she never
came back. But Milena had never been a girl who was
late, and the train caught her. She was shivering one day
long ago when we climbed into an empty car to go visit
Québec City, one of the rare off-duty weekends. It was
then that she spoke to me of trains that frightened her
also. We had that in common. Trains made us mad. Me
in Chicago, where it began, and she, in her country, well
before her. When Milena returned to her country, I
don't know how nor why, she found herself near the rail
line. From her place, she could hear the train go by. Her
daughter, my goddaughter, must have heard the 8:30
train on Sunday mornings, and for many years after her

mother's death. I tried to bring Marina to me. The father never agreed to it. In 2002, she left. She wasn't seen again. She must have caught a train. A train for I don't know where. I often hope that train will transport her all the way here, to me. I often hope she'll knock on my door or appear one night of the full moon at my hospital. I'll show her Québec and then her mother, her splendid mother such as she never knew her. Her Québécoise mother. I'll show Marina everything. And Rose will be happy to meet her. I continue to hope that she'll think to come see me, that she'll find a way to think of me. Not like her mother, not like her ingrate of a mother. Her mother didn't even think to speak to me before catching the train. Nothing, no, nothing. It had been three months since I'd had news from her. Work, life. Life rolls along, as fast as a train. But it's best to be late. To miss the train, let the coach pass. That's what I've done all my life, and there's no regretting it.

I think of destinies. The destinies of Milena, the destinies of Flore, the destinies of Madeleine. I think especially of the uneventuated destinies. Of you, Milena, who didn't grow old, of Madeleine who sank into her banality. It's not hard to predict, really. Madeleine, we could have figured it out. If we had spoken together of the future, Milena and I, if we hadn't stopped at savouring the present, eaten it all raw, we would have lauged imagining what was to follow. To fucking follow.

And of course, we would have got everything right about
Lévesque. Milena and I would have thought of her
professional success, her recognition by political bodies,
her inexorable stupefaction, her wrinkles and pastiness,
swellings of the soul and bent corners pretty much
everywhere. We would have seen all of it. There are
people whose lives are completely laid out. Madeleine's
life line is the highway of idiocy. Yes, Milena and I
would have hit the bull's eye. A direct hit. And we didn't
even know the fat English jackass. But the rest of the
story was all predigested. Ready-made. If we had spoken
of the future, we would have imagined Milena covered
in glory, in her country and perhaps in Africa and
even elsewhere. In a world health organization. Milena
wanted nothing for herself, but this was necessary for her
country, for her father, her dead mother and the whole
tribe, the whole tribe from over there. Yes, we would
have imagined her happy elsewhere. Happy and prolific.
Inexhaustible, fecund. Something killed her. The return
home. The kind husband. The nearby rail line. The
past comes back sometimes. Fifty years is nothing. A
train passes and we return with our kin to Dachau,
Treblinka, Auschwitz, Buchenwald. A train passes and
then we don't want to miss a single meeting. Something
killed you, Milena. And it must have been powerful.
No one could hold you back. You must have thought
it through. Weighed the pros and cons. If only for a

minute, a second... You must have put everything on the little scales. We got such contraptions in our heads. Our brains stuffed with real balances. In brain dissections, it's all one finds. Trays, assay-balances, trebuchets, tares. You'd think that's all we ever did. That we weigh our souls, our decisions, our loves, our joys. You'd think that life is an immense weigh-in, a troubling spirit gauge where everything is scaled, judged. Even the end. Milena had the future to herself alone. She and I would have bet on my premature end, my quick suicide, an automatized autolysis, a grand performance. After having dragged my demented depression all over the place, bandied around my grave, mournful air, I could but suppress myself, sway at the end of a rope, shove myself under a train, a bundle off the end of the pier, play the great love scene, just as the curtain rises. Milena would always say to me that I would end badly, for always raising a hue and cry, never letting go. *Flore, if you carry on like this, destiny is going to strike you, but that's you. Flore, that's the way you are. Like a train speeding toward the nearest precipice.* You're one to talk, Milena. You were talking and you're not talking anymore. And me, I continue my life without unexpecteds, my life that hobbles along, my anesthetized life. How I ran from my birth onward and all for naught. To always be behind in everything, to miss all my meetings. Especially those with death so loudly announced. So much mine. I

finally understood that I had hard skin and a crusty
rind. I ended up glimpsing that, for me, destiny isn't the
one who knocked one childhood night by giving me
an appointment at a later date. Destiny isn't the one I
thought I recognized at first glance. There are a fair share
of imposters and me, I'm the first on the list of living
charlatans. The great usurper of a chance that finally
belongs to me. Well, yeah, it's mine, life, I mean. And
that comes as a surprise.

I'm still surprised when I catch a glimpse of myself
in the mirror to find that I have anything to do with this
woman who will soon, in a not-too-distant future, arrive
at fifty years the way one touches the tip of an infamous
mountain peak. I'm nothing of an alpinist, nothing
of an explorer. Youth was enough for me. I know it
well enough. Why must there be ever and more and
always and then some. Why was it necessary to find out
what aging is? And especially to decay, lemming-like,
gregariously and in bad company? I didn't see it coming,
I didn't pave the way. And now that Mother is dead, I'm
really getting old. I work in usury and forced attrition.
Hackneyed and tatty. The novelty is in my not having
expected it. I'm still flabbergasted as I watch myself carry
on fastidiously with life. Enough for my enemies to be
exultant. For them, it's a piece of cake. I serve them up a
joke on a silver platter. God knows I'm brave... Courage
comes to me naturally... I ooze bravery and I never once

fainted before a corpse or a wound. No, never... But I
think nonetheless and even though I keep my place,
even though I'm often on duty or rather standing at
attention, I know I'm inept. I'm in a serious muddle. I'd
feel better in a big black hole. Rose would get on very
well with Hervé or Julia, her babysitter who picks her
up in the evening because I can't. From now until the
end, I'll have become a bitter apple, a vermouth you spit
up, inconspicuously, when the hostess's back is turned.
There's a rub in my life, it's that it isn't blowing up.
Sometimes it implodes, but the roundabout keeps going
round. Even if there are fewer players and Madeleine
is right there. The days continue their tourniquet.
Tickle you under there. The hours whirlwind and I don't
disappear. The minutes roll, they barrel and collect. I
can't see the semaphores anymore, the road signs that
warn me of the danger of becoming Madeleine or
weighing a hundred kilos, like the fat Englishman with
an Austin belly. I'm getting old in reverse, deadlocked
and ass-fucked by time that grips me. He delivers a
blow, a tremendous clout and I let myself be, I let myself
get fucked. Still, I'm a little bit afraid. But we get on
well enough. Oblivion will inebriate me, it's such a
carnal flower. I've stopped with my bigheadedness. I've
chased away my disposition. That's what skidaddles
with the passage of time. I've stopped speaking of the
slammer when I point to the hospital. I've stopped

saying: "The honcho who reigns over the cemetery is called Madeleine and she's a serial killer." I say nothing more, nothing, nothing, nothing, and nothing again. I'm happy just to operate, my body intoxicated, and to go home at night to get cooked. But I have a steady hand and my eyesight is still good. I open and close the poor hungry flesh of flowering health. I plant orchids in bruised organs and wait for them to grow, I wait for them to grow. There are of course losses. The rootless dead, for whom the graft doesn't take or who can't get used to that fatty soil. I shed a few tears, I have a good cry. I tell myself that's the way it is. No glee. We stagnate anyway, on the earth or beneath the earth, and even in grey ash scattered to the wind. I don't waste my time suffering because of death, the one who arrives too late, the one who strikes too soon. I'm done shrieking. Honour and even justice. I raise my glass to time. Let it do as it will... I have a brand new destiny. I beg, I hope... Entire years in need of redecorating. I sacked my death, there's no point making a big deal out of it. I'm just foul, cowardly, and hardly dangerous at all. And I'll go on, promise, compromise. The days are geraniums, nasturtiums, wild ivy... It will keep climbing, up, always further up. I hope to die of it but not too soon. I'm nothing special. I want a mediocre life. It's my mission, my art, my masterpiece. I'm no longer wanted in this hospital of vampires. I'll eat those bastards up without

even letting them bleed. It's my speciality. Never a
hemmhorage. I'm hematophagous. They'll drain slowly.
We'll croak together, the fat Englishman and me. We'll
plough the horizon. We'll flower the future. Poisoned
clematis, virous azaleas, chancroided rhododendrons,
mycosic lilies, abscessed roses will syphilize the future,
contaminate it good and well. We'll fertilize the soil
of tomorrow with our pathetic existences. The fat
Englishman slowly decomposing. That makes for a lot
of fertilizer, Sir. The world will be infested with new,
utterly rotten species, full of sepsis... I'm up to my neck
in dreck. I'm floundering in feculence and putrid refuse.
There will be no miracle... We're real puppets and we'll
be operative until the end of the show, without looking
for trouble, without making a fine mess. For this, I shoot
myself up in quiet.

At work, they're jackasses, laggards, good-for-
nothings, shitheads, "sodomaniacs," as the writer Céline
says. They want to eliminate me, screw up my system,
fill me with fury, make me sick and fumigant also. But
I play by the rules. I'm chatty in the shabby hallways.
*I went through a bit of a rough patch. But I'm in good
company. Even my brother is here.* They look at me
suspiciously, a sly air about them. They're looking for
an angle to execute me. Is my neck thin enough? There,
could they slice me easily? I don't give anything away.

Or rather I show it all. I always look like I'm singing,
wanting to have a chat. They dream of assassinating me.
It shows in their eyes, in their way of scrutinizing me.
They look at me strangely, sideways, always sideways.
They avoid me, correspond with me by email. It's easier.
Our offices touch, but they prefer to write me to discuss
a patient. Then they would have written proof of my
incompetence. The more courageous among them
stop when I hail them in the corridors. Their voices
tremble, quaver, stutter, but they hope I'll weaken and
feel themselves very strong, in the face of others, not
chicken-hearted, for having responded to my strange
advances. It must be said that they weren't used to such
civility. I never spoke to them. I was making them hug
the walls as soon as they would catch sight of me at the
end of a big alley. The old guard is unforgiving. But
the young are, in fact, worse. They dream of getting
me fired to prove to themselves that they're talented,
that they can have their place, that tomorrow, if they
wanted, they could open the most rotten entrails to
read into their grandiose futures. They want me on the
chopping block, or at very least in prison. If they knew
how to operate, I'd help them with their Forget carnage.
But in butchery, they don't chop up their game as well
as I do. They leave viscera all over the place, and don't
even know what to do with it. Madeleine's the one who
chooses them or her own underlings. And, of course, she

175

only hires more mediocre than she. She hires the paltry, the narrow, the petty. Hope as they might, take pleasure as they will in my defeat, my fall is elsewhere. They can come see me or often avoid me, those hogs, those piglets steeped in hospital pork products, they can suss out the carnage, the cadaver in me, call up evil, implore an end, their hatred doesn't touch me. Their cutlasses are caresses. Of them, I have no fear. They do it in their pants as soon as there's some shit to contend with, an operation gone awry, a patient who's freaking out. Me, I save the day when it isn't even my turn. I pick up the broken pieces and glue it all back together. That's why I chose this dirty job so long ago. Between life and death, I'm not mistaken. I don't hesitate for a second. I never had a doubt. Milena was like me. We have medicine in common. The desire to understand and then to prolong. Prolong the patient, life, at any cost. I'm there and I operate. They are on their guard, wondering where they should look to better see the withering in me. They're human, nothing is to be expected of them. There are those among them who would do Auschwitz all over again, Treblinka. They wait only for that. Nothing stops them. Other than my bad faith, my masked demeanour, my hypocritical face. They end up believing me. I'm the only one laughing. And I laugh scarlet yellow, and I only laugh up my sleeve. I give the impression of peace. I grow old under cover. I hide out among them. I howl with the wolves, the jackals, the dogs. I'm a twilight. I accept the collapse, the comedown, a Punch and Judy existence.

And time passes apace. I'm growing old, it's crazy, and I accept all of it. I stagnate with them and don't dream anymore. Go where? To see whom? The world is everywhere rotten. Madeleine, at least I know her. I can make her suffer, and sometimes bite the dust. The fat Englishman will bite the bullet. With a bit of luck before I do. Maybe there is some justice. I won't attend his funeral. I'll invent a voyage, emotion, friendship. I'll send flowers, something show-off-y enough to display my sorrow, my infinite sadness, how much he mattered to me. I'll send a word to his family, to Madeleine, to praise the dead pachyderm. Works of benevolence, works of malevolence, he was always there, getting his nose in everything. I put it in my will that I don't want that fatso at my funeral. I don't know if he'll have the nerve to show up or whether some devoted friend will have the courage to kick him in the ass, to block his way. I don't want him there. For Mother, I lied to them about the time and the place. Under the guise of confusion, the muddle of mourning. They went elsewhere, I don't know where exactly. They were relieved, I think, not to have to embrace me, to take me into their big gluey calamari arms. They lack courage. But I won't keep killing myself by saying it again. I'm getting old. I accept everything. They'd like to see me pulped, hacked to pieces. But they can't have me. Even if I age ten years every day. Even if I stuff myself full of pills and sail along permanently. I hate them still and will for a good while longer. I'll hate them until the Last Judgement, until they stop believing, those godless people of little faith. I still hate them, but differently. I'm only just learning hatred, but not the hatred that is discharged with a single shot. I'm learning slow hatred.

I'm growing old. That's all.

Eight

YESTERDAY MORNING, I saw Caroline go by. She
didn't look at me. That's how it's been since her niece
died. Sometimes she stares at me, haggard, without
so much as a greeting. Sometimes she barely says
hello, avoiding my eyes. She speeds up. And then,
another time, she'll throw herself into my arms, ask
me to console her, hold her tight, tight. Tells me it's
unbearable, that she doesn't know what to do anymore.
That she misses the little one too much, that her brother
is suffering so much, that it's awful. That she knows
Mother is dead, that she knows what I'm going through.
That she would like to see Rose, but that she can't. That
children hurt her. The mere idea of them wounds her.
She finds it terrible not to have even the slightest bit of
generosity. The laughter of kids in the street is torturous,
the sun stinks, the sky is pestilential. She's a sight
for sore eyes. It's been over five years since Catherine
died. She was only eight. And wouldn't be very old. A
very charming child. Mirthful, good-natured. A giant
leukemia carried her off. Two or three years of struggle.
At that age, that's something. I'm a lucky bastard not
to be an oncologist! A golden girl for not having to
work with little children! That's not my specialization

and it's just as well. I didn't know little Catherine very well. But while she was sick, Caroline asked me to go see her. She knocked on every door, didn't know which way to turn. *Why not go see Flore? She may know what to do...* I'm a doctor, dammit, I should be able to do something... Catherine was a gentle child who could see death coming. In her eyes, one could see that it was there, but she wasn't afraid. For the peanut gallery, her parents, her aunt, the fairy godmother, it was, however, necessary to bluff. Console all her people. Children and death don't go well together. And yet, all those that I have known and who were approaching death were more knowledgeable of things and better able to enjoy their days. My friend Hervé is an admirable guy. I have very few colleagues whom I don't hold in contempt. Hervé saves millions of kids, but he sees some of them die. Often, he comes to cry in my office. Each time a child dies, he is shaken. And he continues. There are others he must care for. There are the parents to follow. The children move him, they reach him. He finds them wonderful. They teach him about death. I don't know how they do it. That profound force, that relationship to life. As though they were simply passing by this world. And just this morning I saw Caroline pass by. She was a wanderer, a shadow, a girl out of place. Nothing belongs to her. Not even the time for a game or a round. She was an unhappy ghost and I barely noticed her.

I'm afraid she'll do herself in. Her brother tells me she
won't, that it's a way of life. She just lost her mother.
The misfortunes accumulate. Her niece isn't coming
back. Caroline waited for her for a long time. After a
day's work, at her door, she would see her. Catherine
would come pet the cats. Caroline lives next door to
her brother. The little one was always there. Now she
is no more and God knows where she is. I bumped
into Caroline and I dreamt of Rose. In my dream, my
daughter was speaking to me of blue-scented flowers.
*Yes I know, Mother, I remember what I tell you in dreams,
every night.* That's what she tells me in the morning,
when I describe my sleep to her. My daughter is a
pythia. A ripening witch. Sometimes she frightens me.
She speaks like a poem. Sibylline words. Very mysterious
words. Sentences that take on meaning, that unfold in
time. A concentrated future comes out of her mouth.
My daughter has a voice from elsewhere, a voice outside
of time. I'm not at the level of my little prophetess. I
don't always know what to do with my soothsayer. This
morning she came into my bed and said: Mother, that's
enough. Let grandmother go a bit. I want some pastries.
We need a celebration full of cakes, chocolates. You have
someone who can do all that for us. I was completely
taken aback. I was completely gaga. I don't know what
to say anymore, when she enters into the quick. *Where
is this coming from, my soothsayer, my angel?* She'll be a

181

writer or a dancer, she promised. Our friend Hervé is showing her the way. Hervé is a great poet. A poet of death. The death of children. And Rose swears only by him and his daughter Anna. They speak in tongues all three of them, they glossolalie. I don't understand a thing and I watch them have a good laugh. Hervé tells me I should put myself to literature more than I do. How much better it would be than meds! That's where he finds consolation. But I don't know how to read. I only know how to spit. I'm like a dragon. I vomit words of fire. Literature is another story! I don't know it. My daughter wants me to live, for us to laugh, to dance. She likes the Crackpot. I think she's exaggerating. Hervé also likes to chat with him. It must be the poetry! The dead, all the rest... I don't understand a thing, and I don't want to understand. I must not be demented enough. There are the poets, madmen who have a screw loose, my daughter, my brother, Hervé, Anna. Those people are birds of a feather. And me, I'm elsewhere, shut into the straightjacket of my vehemence. There's nothing tender in me. I don't even have sweet folly. I'm sad after a few drinks, and too often, also after gloomy medication.

My daughter, my child, do you know that I love you? It begins with your eyes and I lick your lashes. I want them nice and wet, washed of all melancholy. Moistened by the tongue that traces signs onto your sleeping lids. You want me to live? OK, fine... What

must I do? I want to sweep everything aside, destroy
love. Toss the Crackpot out on his ass, along with his
friends. But you ask me to keep everything, to protet my
big brother. You tell me you like him a lot, your uncle,
the German. It's because he often vociferates in the
Germanic language, and you and Hervé laugh quietly.
You don't see that he's mad. That this could end badly.
You tell me he's funny, a big joker. Rose, you want us
to take the train, to speed ahead into the coming days.
Choo, choo. You are my locomotive. I'm the big railway
carriage that has trouble not derailing, that's much too
overloaded. *Choo choo,* that's what you say, and the
Crackpot helps you along, in my orange living room,
to play train, or ocean liner, or airplane, or Russian
rocket. My brother's stories go back to the Cold War.
Rose speaks to me of Gagarin in the Luftwaffe. At first I
wondered where she'd picked that up. Not on the radio
or the television. That's Florent's childhood, it's mine
in storage. Germany, the USSR, time gets all mixed
up. Everything turns to mush. Rose says Gagarin and
giggles. *Gagarin, all gaga gargles in the sky.* Her laughter
is a waterfall. And the Crackpot laughs with her, and
then I don't know how to kick him out. I often wonder
what I'm doing here, I mean in my life. Why you, my
darling, and then why the child? Why play at one's life
with the life of a little one? But it's the sort of thing for
which there is no answer, it's even the sort of question

one mustn't ask oneself, not even once. Because the answer is far too complicated. It brings us back to 'why this' rather than nothing and metaphysical problems I'd rather forget. I'm just a doctor. I'm nothing of a philosopher.

When I was a child, I believed the world was made just for me. That my mother, my two brothers pretended to exist, that everything was a set, that if I turned around fast enough, I'd catch sight of the truth. Looking over my shoulder at top speed became a tic, second nature. They wouldn't have had the time to reset the stage, the inauthentic stage of my existence. One day, after a thousand vain attempts at turning around extremely fast, I wanted to be clear in my mind. I had to intervene, I had to do something. I was five years old. It was time for me to know. I decided to carry out an experiment on my younger brother, Genêt. One evening, I went and found him. I announced to him, as he was falling asleep, that we were all fake and that he alone existed, that life was made of paste-board. *Soon we'll disappear and only you will be left...* I had told myself, knowing him well, that he would admit his misdeeds and cough it up. He would tell me that he, Mother, Florent had all been faking it for years. My little brother burst into tears. He howled with fear. My mother came running. I was punished for a long time. Though convinced of nothing. They were really very good. And God too, who orchestrated it all. Sometimes I believe in God, but it's thanks to Violette, and now Rose. Rose will make me gaga and even Gagarin. Without her, I would have killed my brother, slit the throat of my brand new boyfriend, slain Madeleine just now and made minced meat of the old anesthetist, the pathological Englishman who still wants my head. For Rose, I stay alive. I owe her at least that. And then she doesn't care about death. She still speaks to Violette. She sees her often and has discussions with her and the Crackpot and with Hervé also. They have conversations. It almost frightens me. And then I feel excluded. I don't know how to laugh. I'm dull, macabre. I'm always sorrowful, with tears in my eyes, undone. And with my Rose a lot of the time I have epiphanies, apparitions of life that make sense. Plop, there it is! Plop, it's gone. That's also how I saw Mother. With her, something else happened to me, took place... The world unfurled. Under Rose's charm, it descends toward me, it proffers itself, it gives itself, it falls to me. ·Bing, bang, I take a big hit in the face, from the good lord, and it's fun! Rose turns into a place, a space, in a second. She fills time and serves it to me lukewarm, and a wonderful plate of white porcelain. *But let yourself be tempted, Mother, have some more. This cake of days is made for you. This angel's food cake, it's grandmother who's sending it to you. Close your eyes and have a taste. Fill you mouth full of it.* It reminds me of a story, a children's

185

rhyme that we would repeat all the time: *Hail, Mary, full of grace, the Lord is with thee, blessed art thou amongst women, and Jesus, Jesus...* I don't remember it very well, Rose, or maybe I don't want it to come back. Those were the words of childhood, the ones that tasted good, tasted like the sweetened milk I drank every night, after my prayer. It's better to forget. Kill memory in the bud. Youth was Catholic: a real miracle. More often than not, I hated the good Lord, relics full of worms and the crippled of the world. But sometimes, there were miracles, fabulous things. Communion was divine. I was rustling with happines. God had come. But gently, not harshly. He'd cut off his beard, even shaved. He smelled of aftershave. He smelled priestly. I greeted him with serenity. He resembled an immense cake made of cream puffs, pink sugared almonds, green ones, yellow ones, white, blue, silver ones. A rain of confetti. Thus did he descend from his sky of clouds. That day, I loved religion, baptisms and confirmations, the goofiness of tadpole childhood, the frog-legged years in holy water sometimes scented with orange blossom. *Ribbit, ribbit,* says the past to me, swelling even more. Very small, I smiled at those taking communion, at the virginal whiteness, the unveiled sky, summer Saturdays when witless people get married. I cherished the life that laughed at Fontenay-aux-Roses, in the early sixties, when we would visit an aunt of my mother's. At Sunday mass, the white light descended like a monstrous sweetness. The smell of wisteria mixed with that of the preserves. God had a taste for sugar. I savoured him vanilla-flavoured, in candied fruit and chocolate charlotte. I licked my chops. I kissed him on the mouth and was careful to give him some tongue. Rose, I want so much to cook you up a clafoutis childhood, a profiterole childhood, croquignole, cream-puff, chouquette. From the praline of hours to the nougatine of dreams. For you I desire orangeade souvenirs, a grenadine memory, a chocolate past to bite into, to digest and then one day for you to become a mint cordial. My mother with her violet-water, France with its rose-water, it was also that. And not always the war. There were armistices and even amnesties. I would like to erase the battles, the dead and the horror of this world. I would like to abolish the numbers, senile numbers, sordid repetitions, 14-18, 39-45, those numbers like delayed action bombs that explode in my face fifty years later. I don't know how to go about growing flowers that aren't funeral bouquets. I'm just a belt, a link in the chain, for all of this to continue. And we don't get to decide what continues. At first there was my mother, and now here is Rose. I'm good only for this, transmitting from her to her. But what I pass on, I pass to myself in quiet. I make a baby behind my own back, without understanding what's cooking. I can't even tell whether I've come into this

world for any reason other than the encounter of those
two flowers, my daughter and my mother. It was
obvious that their scents would combine. It's inside of
me that the unavowable perfume was concocted. I was
just a stitch in the jersey of days. And I'm not a little bit
proud. I think that in this case, I take responsibility. But
it took a while. Celebrations can't be improvised. I'm
condemned to life. There are worse punishments. I'm a
hooligan, a scoundrel, a yob of the slums, but I know
the verdict: *Mom, you stay where you are.* Yes, Rose,
you're right. That's what I was telling my mother. And
today, it's my turn to pay, to prepare the great ball and
the waltzes, the soirees, the routs. How beautiful you are
in a tutu, Rose. A little ballerina. You turn so well, how
you can dance. It's the dance of angels and this round's
on Jesus. Look at his pink heart on the superannuated
image. I had a violet tattooed to my buttock and I'll
have a rose drawn on my breast. My body is yours, my
mother, my daughter. I'm just the passage, the tie
between you two who write one another daily, and even
after Mother's death, her burial. Because it goes on. Even
if I don't see how, even if I don't know everything. Thy
will be done, Lord. I am yours. I feel it, you know, and
you too my sisters, my so very periwinkle mother and
my daughter whose colour is so frank, almost acidulous.
I'm a garland between you. My name is girandole, tress
and floral trait. I wrap myself around the two of you,

from you to you, I seed through time. I inseminate the
future. I'm but a passage, maybe even already past. I'm a
wilted flower, fatigued, flagada... But for you, I turn
myself into an insect, a fat incestuous fertilizing
bumblebee, buzzing among the fragile violets to create
new species of infant roses. I parthenogenize from my
mother to my daughter. And here is the work of the
surgeon Frankenstein. In sea blue sheets, I see you
bobbing, Rose. It's a big beach and you ask me to go
there. We leave on a voyage. Often, to change
everything. Your dreams are marshmallows that you give
me to eat. Every morning, when I leave or return, you
tell me a dream. Often, it's Mother who has come to see
you. And I admit I envy what you see in your dreams.
Mother doesn't come to me as often as to you. I don't
know what I did. But the meds, it's true, don't favour
visitations... They chase away spirits, living and dead.
They prevent the traffic between the here and the
beyond. Apparitions are very clear ideas. I did as you
said, Rose. Mother's house is now Florent's. Genêt is in
agreement. The little bugger is so far away... Mother is
dead, I'm a poor orphan. My mother's paradise, her
house, her garden, her great sun-filled greenhouses need
life and why not him... Mother had me promise I'd take
care of everything. But that was before the return of her
forsaken son. I mustn't wrap myself in the lilac shroud of
my dead Mother. I'm not vestal, I'm no priestess. I'm

189

just a doctor, I prolong life. I graft, I take cuttings, I propagate, I multiply. I make a few miracles. There's something of a glorious thaumaturgist in me. I'm ribald, I admit. That's enough... There are prodigies I can accomplish and those I cannot. I know, it's true, a million sleights of hand, of prestidigitation and as many incantations. A real witch. But I have to recognize my limits. To each her work! The Sunset Boulevard where Violette dwelled may well go to her son, the one who left, the one she didn't love. Go figure the how or the why of it. I'm not the one who decides. It's up to life and life, the whore, knows. The entrance, papered with meretricious moiré textiles or better yet, the rose crystal chandelier of the entrance illuminating the house already suffused with sun do not belong to me. Sunset is a real greenhouse in which, during the last years of Mother's life, I was able to cosset my love for her with each visit. But I, Flore, am not there anymore. It's Florent, the dingo, who will make his nest in that sometimes smothering cocoon where it does me no good to live anymore. I had Mother alive, I leave her to him dead. This is all so violent, but I can't do better than this. Life makes you sweat blood. And frankly, he has suffered. I don't know how he'll make out with the flashy decor, all the kitsch Mother is bequeathing to him. In flowers, Mother wanted artifice, pyrotechnic illusion. Her bouquets were rockets that exploded in the sky, they

were explosions of colours, cries. What will my brother,
the Crackpot, do with Mother's outmoded furniture, the
coquettish couches, the wilted rugs of that polished
dwelling, of that rutilant house? I've so seldom been
back since the funeral. I wanted to sell it, but I didn't
have the courage... It's best not to succumb to the
mausolean, I have nothing to stuff. At the end of her
life, Mother had become a master in the art of
mummification, of herself and others. You've got to
admit that people, as they age, discover themselves to be
taxidermists, talented taxidermists. On Sunset, we found
photographs everywhere, hangings that weren't too worn
but were very discoloured, lacklustre, faint. Even the
house cat had taken on the air of a dried up Pharaoh.
Mother liked canned goods, things that could be
preserved, immortalized. We often end up like that.
Soon, very soon, when the years ring hollow, when the
hours hammer the present by marking the countdown,
I'll have to think to throw everything into the garbage,
without buying anything again. When I feel myself
croaking, I'll go breathe in the Ganges and its
malodorous smells, I'll travel to where time is on the
blink and doesn't seek progress. It's best to disorient
oneself after a certain age. I'm not attached to anything.
Mother often said it was so. And yet Mother, your
objects, I didn't want to let them go. But I'm not a
sanctuary. Things continue. I don't know how.

When I go into your haunt, Mother, it's the ballet of ghosts. I just want to forget. I just want my name. And not my father's. There's nothing left here. Mother isn't beneficent, a beatific, a saint. Sunset isn't Bernadette or Thérèse's shrine. Montréal is not Lourdes, Lisieux nor even Nevers... We don't tread on the past, on millenial tombs over which time passes. Here, I've got to say, it doesn't smell of war in the same way, that's why Mother and her sisters came to America, that's why thirty years ago Florent crossed the Atlantic to transplant himself into European soil. That one is a war flower, he only grows in muck. More than anything he doesn't want to forget the battles. He doesn't miss a beat. Me, I want to forget and ditch everything. The meds help, of course. Giving Mother's house to Florent isn't bad either. I'm not a beneficiary. So it will go to him. He can have time. I'm relieving myself, alleviating myself. Fuck, it's not light at all.

When we were children, we shared everything. Flore and Florent, the twins... Abundant capitulum, bursting corymb. Pistil and stamen: those were our secret names. Our daily incest. Our botanic loves. Years separated us, but that didn't change a thing. We were very similar. Two flowers out of the same soil. From the belly of Violette we bloomed. Born the same day, a June 16th that repeats itself, that knocks a second time over the coursing years, we were tied by chance to returning

seasons, summers that turn up again. Out of this,
Violette made our destiny. The seeds once sewn into
Mother's body brought to light vegetal children, weedy
kids. She was very proud of us. *And they don't have the
same father!* Me, I didn't like it one bit. I know that
Genêt, my little brother, suffered somewhat from it. He
was born in autumn when the flowers look drawn. He
was a cast-off: an exceptional growth, a yellow bush, a
climbing plant that scales and extends. Real vegtation.
He got on better with life, I think. Who can know such
things? But that's what he always says. He never thinks
of war. And as for flowers, he eats them in salads in very
chic restaurants that he frequents with groups, clusters
of trendy artists. Crinch, crunch, croonch. He masticates
the floral and even digests the stems. He's a very fine boy
who isn't moody. At least not every day. It must be said
that Florent and his sister swiped everything,
columbines, melancholy, sweet pea sadness, clusters of
suicides, copses of madness. There was nothing left for
the youngest. They'd stolen it all. When they were
children they made eyes at one another, they gave one
another graces, strokes, canoodles, caresses, tickles, pets.
It degenerated fast, degraded presto. *Pipi, caca. You tickle
me, tits, cunt and cock.* The great sexual comedy, the big
circus of stroking, the tragedy of copulation, the I-lick-
you-you-lick-me-stop-that-hurts-oh!-ok-carry-on-if-you-
want-to. It's like that, we're the same. And then

193

afterwards, shame, because there is no innocence. For humans, pleasure is a sort of ill-being. You're like a vegetable, you plunge without warning into the animal and into the beast, without the beauty. I'm three years old. A gorilla awakens in me. I see him beating his breast. When I get undressed, he's still there, perched on some wardrobe, ogling my ass. It's not just Florent, I'm the one who's orang-utan-ing myself, turning into a monster, an anthropopithecus, a ravaging macaque with a striped ass. Life becomes vulgar, I'm quick to my base instincts. I'm Florent in age, and in coital flesh. Childhood smells of seed, of glans, of cyprine, and in a flash, I'm aware of roses, cabbages and storks that mount one another from behind if you please, slipping one on. Rip-roaring ass-fucking, the ticklish glory hole. At eight, I know everything I need to know. Everyone closes their eyes to our childhood games, our silliness, charming puerility, our innocent souls. We sleep together and fornicate acrobatically. I'm disgusted, but I forget it post-haste. The worlds are closed, hermetic, hot greenhouses that allow a variety of moments to grow. I breathe the air there is. I don't make a fuss. I sniff pleasure and by the same token I breathe in my innate stain. I would never have been pure. There was always a blur, a haze, static in my candid head. I was never an idiot, I mean blissfully so. I only engender doubles and duplicity. Contradictory things, paradoxical ideas. Desires to put an end to things

and especially to persistence. It takes as long as it takes,
but longer than roses, so much longer than a single
summer. And then the years pass, I'm sick of it and more
sick, I scream, I bite, I fight. I don't want anymore of my
brother and my mother the accomplice. It seems to me
that she knows everything and doesn't talk about it. She
wants those two flowers to graft on to one another, to
grow together and point in unison toward an ecstatic
sky. I see my mother as a worm-eaten acolyte, listening
at the door, to the fraternal frolicking, the somersaults of
her seed. I am mistaken, I screw up, I fantasize, I get it
wrong, I sink into loose soil. Later, Violette will tell me,
once Florent has left, that she could not, no, never,
imagine her children... She'll blame herself a lot and cast
the blame onto him. Mothers often lie to themselves,
and I'm the first among them. With my child, Rose, it's
clear that I give over to denial, scotomization... You
don't have to be a great fakir, a seasoned dervish to see
that I'm playing the ostrich. Only, magician that I am, I
don't know what I'm making disappear anymore.
Abracadabri, abracadabra! Flore's wand has struck once
again! Of course we would rather our children not
become bitches in a sexual circus. And I step into the
ring! And I perform my best number! Acrobat, clown,
dancer, lion and Bengali tiger tamer, rider straddling
Sorrel mares, tightrope walker of the soul, gymnast of
feelings, humiliated jester, wounded who must put on a

good face against misfortune, good-hearted, we play every part in this musical chairs. Let the ding-dong begin! Because it starts up again and it even fornicates, it waddles, it wriggles, it keeps it coming in the sacrificial corrida of human loves, of polluted loves. I would dream of sparing my daughter all of this, of not exposing her when she's young to this grotesque courtship, this burlesque rutting. The display case of the senses, the offering of bodies. I started young. That has its advantages. At ten, everything already seemed to me to be in vain. I came very quickly. That's what I'm left with from that period. I'll have to learn to delay pleasure. I'm into mass consumption. For fear of missing the train. Yes, I'd like for Rose to be spared my past. Stupor and sweet nothings, the sibilant death rattle of cavernous passions, puerile crushes that always end with a hand down someone's pants and a quivering bed. It wasn't a trauma. I don't want to give the impression that I'm ruined, damaged, spoiled. Florent and me, when we played at being flowers, when we were pollinating one another, when we were *making catleya,* to say it with Proust whom we hadn't heard of at the time, we didn't cause one another lesions, wounds, indelible keloids. It's simpler than that. We came through much better than that. I'm not the way I am because of my older brother. Everything goes back much further. The origin is lost in the mists of time. But at ten years old, I wanted us to

stop. And it pissed him off. We even stopped being
chummy... There was embarrassment. I remember. We
had been too close. And then that imagined twinning,
that pulp fiction, that rosewater story was very
oppressive to me. That's where all the harm comes from.
I wanted to free myself, break the yoke of fraternity. As
for purity, children have none. Very quickly, they are
tortured with having handled one another's organs.
Don't think they give it a second's thought during the
day. Desire comes, it goes. A bit of nastiness. We're soon
accustomed to human decline... I carried the fracture
within. But I carried it solo. And not with Florent, my
twin torn from my living flesh. I wanted to undo myself
from that leech. I was nonetheless able to, but he
resented me for it. I've got to admit, it fucked him up a
bit, this business... When he could play a dirty trick on
me, he cocked up my life, he gave me a bad name to all
his little friends. Adolescence was rebellious. Blows
below the belt. He called me a dyke. I didn't deny it. It's
true that I have often been a dyke, also true that I
experienced everything that was alive. I'd had my share
at the well of incest and even my full... Finished! Basta! I
think I gave plenty... Others could have it off with it.
That's what I told myself, loudly and then less loudly. In
the sordid alleys and on the wide boulevards. Brothers
are real pissants. They're bloody irritating. If we let them
get away with it, we'd just be their thing. At around the

age of ten, I lashed out, I fought back. I wanted to think of myself a bit. Florent's nuzzling, his infatuations and his fits of anger too, his bouts of possessiveness, his stormy effusiveness, his urges to em-bastille me in the violet family, I couldn't stick them anymore. I wanted to puke when he made a date with me in the evening, snickering. I think it was his beard, his hairy pubis, his thin moustache that did it for me. I found him repulsive. A real man-made truck. It was becoming imperative: it had to end. My door had a gleaming silver lock. I found my bed again. How I loved my bedroom! The soft sheets and my own fingers on myself. The child in me was dead. Farewell, little one! I no longer had to wax my older brother's boots nor give him a flaccid blowjob at night, by the light of the moon. I don't think kids have lives other than this. Like it or not, time moves on and life goes as I shove you along. A real fist fair... We take what passes and even what passes with difficulty. We get ideas in our head. And then there's more to it than that. I had moments of freedom. Sometimes I would go stark naked in the garden, I would dance the carmagnole, a frenzied polka, I would spin like a top and then fall suddenly like a sack of potatoes. And wham, I put my buttocks in the earth, I screwed my ass to the ground, wriggling every which way. I was trying to fill my vagina, my anus with slightly moist earth. A real pleasure! The black, fresh earth is much better than my brother. Sometimes, of course, a plump spider would rush at me. I'd start to scream, my mother would come. She didn't ask questions. She laughed heartily and thought I wanted to plant myself in the soil like a little white, virginal tree, so pure. After my incestuous fevers, I continued for several years more to copulate in the garden, to let myself be sodomized by humus or terra rossa, or the muddy shit of a late spring. Then I shared this Eden with makeshift friends and little lady killers.

My brother wasn't much to me anymore, barely a memory. I know next to nothing about the next part of the world, the lovemaking of that blessed Florent. He took drugs. He tried everything: he certainly looked like it. A girlfriend told me so, on one of our wasted days, our days of drink and mucky gardening. Florent's brain must have taken a blow. He burned several brain cells. In my view, the more important ones. There's something in him that's seriously unhinged. After his departure, I also learned, through my adolescent years, of his extravagances and ravings. His youthful antics. In Québec City, in his father's family, he hung out with a demented girl: Blanche Comtois. She'd lost her head and imagined herself to be the Immaculate Conception. Apparently my brother had knocked her up. But we're not too sure, especially since Comtois masturbated all summer long by rubbing her breasts on the front steps. She let out loud cries. Florent had liked it. One Sunday morning, he'd approached her. They were thick as thieves. Still, she had to abort. And my brother, back at square one, fell back on his own cousins on his father's side. No connection to me. Our kinship ends there. After, I don't know. Rumors, gossip, some background noise. It was also sworn to me that he was a homosexual. Is it even true? Someone mean told me that, a boy I wasn't interested in, that I didn't want anything else to do with, and who also called me a dyke. *It's in your genes,* telling me my brother came on to him one night when they were playing Werewolf. But I don't know anything more than this. And I didn't want to know. Things turned bitter. They weren't going at all well between Florent and me. I couldn't stand him... Sometimes, from time to time, a conversation, a reminiscence of our complicity. But it didn't last, it quickly collapsed, and turned sour. There was no way to revive the corpse of childhood. No way to pick up where we'd left off. Incests like ours don't happen every day. Coupling false twins don't come in droves. But I don't think we're the exception, the rare, the accidental. People drone on today about Sophie's Misfortunes, and Isabelle's and Flore's and Florent's. My sadness doesn't come from there. It was born before me. And even before my brother. Obviously, I don't leave that asshole alone with Rose. There are always other people, folks who keep an eye out, friends who adore him. I don't go looking for

trouble. I'm even on my guard. I want a less morose
childhood for my Rose. But I'm not blaming anyone
and I have no regrets. If Florent hurt me, it's because of
the ringing bells that ring and ring and the trains
especially. From Chicago, USA, from the madness he
filched from me, that he made his own. There was
nothing left in my head, other than that endless
choochoochoo, a long whistle, a persistent tinnitus that
made me yell my whole life long to cover it over. I had
to shriek to avoid hearing it, shout at everyone, bell,
wail. I felt as though Florent had nicked the meaning of
all those rotten noises sabotaging my brain.
Choochoochoo in my head, and then I forgot why... A
rhythm, a cadence, a precipitation... War that hums,
that buzzes encephalically. The skull turned to mush, the
cortex damaged. One day a locomotive entered my
dome and has never resurfaced. I had to distract myself
to keep from going mad. Vituperation, fulmination,
discontent. An uproar of thunder so as not to hear
myself. I spat on everyone and against myself to boot.
With all that expectorating, my lungs were weary and I
lacked pytalin. For thirty years, I dragged my rage, my
anger, my discontentment around just about
everywhere. I also bandied my great indifference. For a
renegade brother I never saw again. And then the
brother comes back and childhood beckons me. Not the
childhood rewritten with Violette, my little Mother of

my own, but the I'm-getting-a-real-faceful-my-brother-makes-me-sick childhood. There's my mother who dies and all I can do is change myself. And keep a distance from the frenetic, libidinous, salacious brother. Push madness far away from the family, the tribal wreck. Childhood is stuck in my throat and I don't want it, don't want that sad, fragile Flore with her worn-down misfortune. My mother was mine, but dead, I don't want her anymore. You want her, Florent? You like corpses, remains and even crumbs. OK, you can have her. You've come back for that. To have her and have her again. Well I'm making a gift of her to you. Just don't bring back our incestuous love, our twinship, our hallucinations. It's been kept under lock and key for thirty short years. I don't want it. You can keep everything for yourself. Mother's house is yours, my brother. Yours by rights. Me, I'm rejecting it. I had my share and much more. Of my little Mother, I benefited. It was a great joy in fact that you had split... Thank God and thank you. It's time for the count. The choochoo is disappearing in my head, getting lost off in the distance. The pills are helping me a lot to erase that noise. I give unto Caesar what is Caesar's. The embalming of the past, the sustenance of dementia. You'll manage all of that. You'll dust off time and give Mother a good brushing. I'm passing that legacy off to you. That's what you'll get. I'm becoming a notary. Rose is pushing me to

give, to forgive. Let's repair the misdeal. It's time for
New Year's gifts. OK, I absolve you of everything, OK we
can see one another. We'll put up with one another, I
hope, not too often. I remember as a child having
wished for my death. I wanted to be able to taste my
own rot. The capers, the somersaults, the carnal scuffle,
the screwy spin, the little sex games, I think that all
saved me. Life is imperfect, it squirms with worms,
lugworms, ants, termites and big fat rodents. But I also
see larvae, chimeric caterpillars, chrysalids that turn into
all pink tinkerbells, river nymphs that metamorphosize,
anamorphosize, explode. One needs something to hang
on to. And as a child, I clutched at my Mother, but
Florent as well. Joy, naked bodies, hot bodies in the
night. The nyphomaniac serenade of childhood, the
polymorphous perversion of which the great Freud
speaks. I allowed myself other forms. Often, I was a
tadpole, but I was also a buzzard. I hopped like a frog
and made myself into a duck, perhaps ugly and small,
but I took my flight when a mean hunger approached in
my woods. I lived like a white maggot, a fly in shit, in
mire, dung, decomposition, but I also knew how to be
the princess and the pea, reject boredom, unpleasantries,
take myself for someone else, the person I was as well.
Childhood is terrible, a real violent poison. I know of no
antidote. We all go through it. The pain of growing up,
the fear of remaining caught in the snares of smallhood,

of insignificance. There is no answer. Life passes and that's all. You want something, sure, and then its opposite. To be loved all your life by your mother, your family, and take off from there, lickety split. You don't know what is in you, you live in a haze. Strange feelings you don't know how to read properly. Childhood is like that. Afterwards, we pretend. We make decisions, it's black, it's white, it's cut and dried, it's blood red. But as a child, childhood gets us right in the sucker. Bang. And contradictions. Boom, boom. No way to decide, to say yes or no. We're close to limbo. We're still hesitating between the magma behind us and the one spread out in front. Children rock between the before and the beyond, between the here-and-now and the I'm-not-here. *It's not a big deal,* said little Catherine to her parents. *Death's not a big deal. A long time ago, I was there. And you'll come meet me soon. In a maximum of one hundred years, we'll be reunited. The plants are much older. Millions of years. You've got to see them. Death isn't fun because we're humans. But you have to think more broadly. In light-years, like God, like time, like physicists... Then you feel better, you understand that it all has meaning, despite everything... You just have to find it.* Caroline sometimes remembers the words of her little niece. Catherine had promised that after she died she would speak to her otherwise. That the flowers, the wind, the little birds, the flies would bring her news of her and of great big paradise.

Don't kill the ants, my aunt, the ones that come into your house and that you exterminate with your Easy-Off. I'll come see you disguised as an ant. You'll take me into your hand. You'll recognize me. Catherine cried sometimes. But often she laughed. *We'll stop at death when it gets here.* Catherine remained a child forever. Me, I killed little Flore and I have to make do. Growing up is putting oneself tragically to death. Not as dramatically as the dead in their coffins, the dead that suddenly stiffen, and are rapidly buried. But it's a slow slow gentle gentle agony. We forget over time. Children remind us of it. That's what they're there for, isn't it? To speak to us of the future, the future that always rings false, that tolls like a knell, but opens its arms. Rose I want your life to offer itself to you, ugly, clumsy, borrowed. It's awkward, I know, but it's not bad either. You'll do what you want with your child-death. You'll determine your own sacrifice, the one that will one day bloom in you to assassinate ideal childhood. Me, it's been a long time since I did in the candid virgin, Flore. Otherwise, I'd have died of all that virginity. Too heavy to carry in an overripe world. I admit that in that crime I was given lots of help. I say a big thank you! Childhood will only last as long as my Rose does. The future is yours, my girl. Do with it what you will. To Florent, I flog the house. And me, I'm the conveyor, the transfer, the transmission. Between you and Mother, there will only be me! Taken together, the three of us make up the divine Trinity!

Nine

LIFE RINGS AT three fifteen in the morning, in the
night, a Saturday. I answer right away. I don't think
twice. I don't know whether I love this life. But I answer.
That's the way it is. My cook is in my bed, his legs
wrapped around my body, as he concocts a future for
me, making another meal out of me, preparing the
pleasure he'll serve me for breakfast. My daughter is in
her bedroom, her dreams entangled with mine. The
loves are asleep, the loves are somnolent. The loves are
gathering strength. They'll need it. May nothing, more
than anything, come and trouble their slumber. May the
loves sink into nocturnal oblivion. How sweet it is not
to be there... And yet life is ringing. Ring, ring. I answer.
Hello... Hello, of course. I'm a surgeon. I don't have the
right to sleep. No slumber for me. There is no
intermission. The acts follow quickly, the scenes straddle
one another. It just carries on. I sleep with my eyes open.
You never know. Life can ring or else knock me out. As
it happens, it's ringing me now. Life rings, it summons
me not to forget. I'm here! I'm here! Not to worry! I'm
all ready, well disposed to operate. Give me a body. To
open, to close up. I know my work, and can handle a
needle with dexterity even while sleepwalking. I've never

slept well. I was always afraid it would ring in the night.
With the time difference, something could happen. In
France, in the morning. It would have awoken us in the
middle of the night. I always kept watch over France,
my mother's whole family. They died little-by-little,
gently, ringing and ringing again. I'm the one who
answered, who would wake Mother. I was able to make
a vocation out of my fabulous insomnia. A job in which
night is made for slogging away. Emergencies don't wait.
When you've got to go, I go. Someone's got to. I can't let
someone who's had an accident croak, or an
appendicitis, or even some brawler who's being bled like
an ox by an old rusty knife. Life rings, I go. I get up
pronto. I'm a good soldier. Always ready for battle. The
battle against death. And I often win. So, I answer. But
tonight, it's terrible, it isn't the hospital. Even as I pull
on my jeans, I can't even rise up against Madeleine who
ought to be taking care of what's going on in surgery
and all my tours of duty. I can't condemn the Lévesque
in the middle of the night. She can snore in peace.
There's much worse. It isn't the telephone. It's the
doorbell. The Canadian Secret Service. Florent's been
acting out. So they say. Sentences I don't understand.
But several words strike me. The German Consulate...
Hostage-taking... impeccable German. I don't believe
my ears. He wants to blow everything to smitherines
and is asking for nothing. He's talking about 45 and 14-

18, Berlin, Hitler and D-Day. Does this sound familiar
to me? Were our parents Germans? I'm made to follow
these hefty men who are bombarding me with questions,
enjoining me to leave with them immediately. Is he
dangerous? What does he do in life? We're already on
our way. The suspect let slide that he had a sister. The
interpreters are translating. They are granting meaning,
too much meaning to that which has none. *My little
sister Flore is the surgeon Forget. She'll understand when
everything blows. She knows.* So they found me. What do
I know? Am I his accomplice? The car is zooming along.
We're rushing. Vroom, vroom. I think of Moscow. Of
those female human bombs, killers before death, their
bellies fat with dynamite, pregnant with horror. I think
of the Chechnyan Erinyes, tragic, so tragic, who wept
imagining they would have the hide of several poor
someones. I can see those Eumenides, those vengeful,
agglutinating Parcae, who agglomerated in murder. I am
haunted by those comrades, those disconsolates, those
reapers who, in their black apparel, resemble crows,
birds of great misfortune. They are at my sides in the
very car. They envelop my most macabre thoughts with
their veils. I hear them shriek and snicker, voraciously.
They want my hide and Florent's. Those vile vultures
want to peck out my eyes and have their way with my
corpse. They've determined the hour and also the place
where it will end for me and for him. I watched them

closely tonight on the TV. My God, how they frighten
me with their cause, their dead. They were admirable.
All prepared to die and carry several hundred people
with them in their flight. They were duty-bound,
something grand. Me, I belong to the race of traitors.
I've mourned every cause. I tinker, I tamper. I live in
mediocrity. I've already spat some. But that was a long
time ago and it wasn't much. Trifles, whatnots.
Bagatelles, nothings. No Russian theatre to disembowel
in blood, no school of children to eviscerate, no bomb
on the belly to go badaboom. I'm fighting with myself.
That's enough. So, I hate them, those press-ganged
women. How I hated that mother, on the TV once
more, who was exhorting her own to send their sons to
certain death. They live in Palestine and demand justice.
Yes, yes, it's justice and they're right, the cause is
authentic, there's no doubt. But is any thought given to
the fact that they're pushing their children into the
beyond, vitiating them, convincing them to die? Not
shedding a tear as they say goodbye to the ones they had
in their bellies, the ones that grew in them, to what
came out, armed, oh how hardened in their evil entrails,
their cruel cunts? One morning, they are filming the
solemn farewells. They are returning to God what he
offered as a gift. I don't find that polite. I don't find that
human. There is assassination in it. There is some Medea
in the air. And here they are, these women who

surround me, embrace me. I don't want anything to do
with them. Go away, Psh! Psh! Let go of me at once ...
What do you want with Flore? Why torment her?
Because she blasphemed and set fire to Joan of Arc?
Because today she renounces her expectorations of
yesteryear? Because the sacrifice is something of the past?
It's with Mother. Buried for a brief time. Very good
riddance, and I'm not in mourning. Life is much too
strong. I want her. She grows back often, and from
nothing. I accept her, I pray to her, beg her to make me
believe in her. Around me, in the car moving at break-
neck speeds toward the German Consulate, are all these
men in suits, men who are powerless to reassure me.
And then there are these women, these invisible
jackdaws who flutter and strike my head. *Your brother is
sacrificing himself. And you, my little darling? Are you
really going to do nothing? You therefore accept everything?*
Causes, I have none. I'd be fine with immolating myself,
blowing my brains out, being detonated, signing
Kalashnikov, but for whom, for what? I have a hard time
imagining what good death can do. Perhaps instigate the
growth of several flowers in the cemetery, generously
nourish somewhat sterile soil. Death is a whore and
must be fought. The veiled rooks are going tss, tss in my
head. *You're going to pay, girl, for believing in nothing.
You'll be Antigone, nothing more, nothing less. You'll call
death and she'll come at last.* The car arrives. It's a dance

of headlights, dams in the night. The Consulate is surrounded. There are three hostages. A security guard, a housewife, and the Consul who works here at night. Florent is negotiating, parleying, parlementing, he's gabbing in German with the Canadian police. He's telling them they've got to win back the war. They must continue to fight and avenge their family. They've got to land over there, eliminate everyone. All you have to do is look at what they did to the Jews. Suspicion is utmost. He's wearing a bomb and a detonator, three reliable submachine guns and dynamite... Yes, yes, he's sitting on it. He talks, talks, talks again, insults, assaults. He's given to anathema and imprecation. It's enough to terrify anyone. But me, I'm used to it. I tell them he speaks French, that it's even his language. I also tell them that I really had no idea he knew German so well. That I want to speak to him on the telephone and that I also want to go in there. My brother doesn't frighten me. Not like this. How often did I tremble for fear of being him, of becoming a vociferating madwoman, a sanguinary voice incapable of articulating nothing more of reality? I was always so afraid of waking up one morning, thinking it was '16 or '42 and and having to play out my life through a German shell while avenging the Jews and the amputees. Our family stole our time. It bequeathed the war to us and it's not easy... How does one forget what one hasn't experienced? They call my brother. He answers, almost jubilant. He's happy to talk to me. Even in French. I'm the only one around here who can gibber in his language. *It's chock full of Jerries, sister. You've got to howl with the wolves to be heard and they only understand Nazi barking, even if they pretend to understand French. Oh yes, they are clever!* With me, it's easy: *the mother tongue.* And he's not mistaken. Mother's language, that's what we're speaking, and with her accent, the accent of the war years. He's happy to hear it. For him, it's a real joy. *You know, after all this time, it feels pretty good.* We saw one another two nights ago. He was playing with Hervé, Rose, the dog, the cat and with my red-headed cook who was happily messing around. But he doesn't remember. He remembers nothing. That rascal's no Forget. He's a real Létourneau. A turnip head with a bird's brain. No memory for things. I mean yesterday. Only the war occupies him. Fucking Occupation... His only memories date back sixty-three years. He's not in this world. He's just come back from thirty years of exile. He hopes to tell me about his life and his past. *But first, to work! We've got to get back at those Germans, once and for all. Be done with them.* And he's going to be the one to do it. I don't know fear. I've never known it. Except for the fear of going mad, of Germany, one day, invading my brain. That shit's happening to him... My mother gave "that" to her three children. But today it's Florent who's going to destroy Germany! He can't take the war anymore, the Germanic victories, the sound of airplanes, the train, in this delirium... He's the one who copped everything of the madness of time. I'm not safe, certainly, from battiness, the tribe run amok, but I haven't reached that point. I convince the police that I can go in. The men are suspicious of me: the hospital is called, information is collected, to find out who I am. Now they're satisfied. They find this business risky, but it's my brother after all and he wants me with him. He can kidnap me too, and open my throat. We're in '44, in France or Germany. The police officers don't understand that this is his motive. He's nothing like a terrorist. My brother's a poor wretch and I should have spoken to him, asked him sooner what he'd done with the past thirty years. But I didn't want to know. I didn't want to know him. It's biting me in the ass. It serves me right. I cross the police lines, the human barriers, the official barricades, and the women in black trail me, snickering. The bitches throw stones at me, pull my hair, pinch the skin of my legs and bite my cheeks. They take it out on my body, my soul, my life, and happily, they insult me, blaspheme and scratch my face, throwing fine sand into my eyes. They threaten the worst. I chase them away like flies. I kill them with my hands. They don't even die, they shriek and return, landing on my mind which they abscond. I'm not listening to you, hard, evil women! I want to save my brother and those three poor people.

I'm not accepting death's arrival. And I'll fight some
more. You can laugh, you can titter, tie yourself in knots.
You're really ugly and I'm not surrendering to you. I'm
advancing toward the consulate and not listening to you.
My brother's calling me.

He's in the basement with three hostages. They look
bewildered, a bit mortified. *What am I doing there? I'm
an accomplice.* The young Portuguese guard doesn't
understand German and the cleaning lady, a small
chubby redhead doesn't know what this crazy story is all
about. Only the Consul sees that Florent is acting out.
But the more she talks, the more he thinks she's the
enemy. I get there, quickly size up the situation, the
stakes, the mistakes and the misunderstandings. The
morbid consequences, the tragic blunders, the
departures and distractions of sense. I go straight to my
brother who really looks potted. I see people like him at
the hospital, for sure, green ones and unripe ones, I see
every variety, but this, really, I've got to say that Florent
did an excellent job... He looks ecstatic. He's jubilant.
He must be hearing voices and even opera, divine music.
He's smiling at the angels. He's pleased with himself.
He's taking stupid pleasure in his success. For him, this
is a great success, everything he's just done. I can be
proud of Florent and the whole family can admire the
grandiosity, the genius, the giant. There are bravos and
hurrahs in his head. Loud bravissimos, encores and

encores... There is applause on all sides, they're bringing
the house down. He's being carried triumphantly,
endlessly ovationed. He looks happy. I'd put my fist in
his face if I didn't hold back. Without missing a beat, I
ask him at very least to let the Portuguese guard and the
little, round redheaded woman who aren't even German
go. He's says it isn't true, they're tricks played by the
Jerries, spy tactics which pass them off as someone else.
*You don't know what they're like, those people. I lived
among them for over twenty years. You can't even imagine
what they're capable of... Concentration camps are small fry!
But yes, they do much worse! You wouldn't believe it...
Monsters such as these you won't find anywhere on earth,
not even in books. I know, I've read everything. They stuck
electrodes to me and played around in my head. Without
even opening my skull. That way I couldn't lodge a
complaint. They're really brilliant. You're a surgeon, aren't
you? You know it's not possible. But over there, all the way
over there, there's technology. I married a woman, one of
theirs, a Dalida. She was on their side, and me, I resisted
her. I got their game, and hers to boot. She had me
hospitalized, but I didn't stay. Several years, no more.
Enough to make one mad. But they won't get me. Someone
else, sure, might have lost his mind. But you see, you just
have to resist surrender. Understand the enemy. You put
yourself in his place, and then you get everything. That's the
job! This way I was able to know that the war wasn't over.*

*That they had their plan and that destruction was
imminent. In fact, they pretend to be fat and happy,
producers of saurkraut, pleasant schools, and call themselves
Europeans. That's all hogwash, a scam, for show. They carry
on as before and Jews disappear and the young enlist and go
into the S.S. but it's camouflaged. They've got good hiding
spots. Hitler isn't dead. But it isn't just him. It goes back
well before. With Bismarck and everything else. I studied
history. I read tonnes of books. I can think like them. It's
hard, but I'm getting there. So afterward, it was hard to
come back. My wife over there almost had me. She's a slut, a
German hen. Kot, kot, kot, in German. I let myself get
taken in sometimes. I was a pure German. I became cruel,
dominating, Nazi. I really had to fight, rebel and then their
psychiatrists drugged me. They injected doses of German or
Austrian thought into me. I read Kant, I read Nietzsche,
Freud, Hegel, everyone. They played music for me.
Beethoven, Mozart et tutti quanti. There was goodness in it,
I could discover something. Their diabolical plans, their
desire for revenge. It was just to understand, just to be like
them. On my own, still, I was able to deprogram myself.
Not easy. I'm tough. But at the hospital, I tell you, they were
really good. They shoved German culture down my throat
and when I went off it, there was no hesitation: presto, the
straightjacket. Pills, that's all manageable. But the ingestion
of philosophy isn't easy. And I couldn't vomit. They made me
digest it. My brain was being Germanized. No way to*

avoid it. I was able to get transferred to France in extremis.
In fact, I ran away. I found myself on the square of Notre-
Dame-de-Paris one Saturday morning. The cops picked me
up and put me in Maison-Blanche. A sanatorium. That's
what those things are called, but I didn't mind Maison-
Blanche. You see, it smelled of America. I played it USA,
big shot presidential. Hell, the Yankees saved us! Even if
they're a bit weak, they believe in redemption, in
reunification and all that bullshit. They want to make
peace, but how can that be, in the middle of a war? Gotta
fight, get banged up, set bombs. Ferdinand asks me to.
Ferdinand tells me to go. So I came here and I saw big. I
swear it's gonna blow. I'll avenge the evil they did to
Mother, and also the evil inflicted on Ferdinand, Flora, all
of Normandy, the whole of France. I want Ferdinand's leg
back, and Alsace-Lorraine and the lives of a good number
of people. That, they can do. Yes, they have the technology to
resuscitate the dead. You're a surgeon, sister, but they're way
ahead of you. In Germany, they don't operate anymore. I
swear, I saw it with my own eyes. But they hide the whole
caboodle. They don't breathe a word of it. They keep it for
themselves. The Jews are vanishing into thin air. But no one
talks about it. Shh, shh! It's a secret! Mum's the word and
lips sealed. At the hospital in Baden-Baden, during the day,
it was still okay... But at night, how they howled! Belling
like calves! It was the Jews of course, but they kept it hidden.
Lies... Sweetnesses... Fibs! Hogwash! And well-seasoned at

that... From midnight to four in the morning I could hear them. They were being tortured to death. And then in the morning, finished. Order fell back into place. As though nothing had happened. I knew what they were doing with the pieces of bodies. And Ferdinand's leg they were messing around with. They insulted me endlessly, they wouldn't let go of me. I escaped, went to France. There was Notre-Dame, Maison-Blanche, and then freedom. I often went to visit Ferdinand and flower Flora properly. Those two were crying for revenge. "You've got to bite the Boches. We want our leg back." Given especially that it continues. I'm happy to let the false guard and the redhead go, OK, if you want. But they're liars, you've got to understand. They're Germans. They're pretending not to get a thing, zilch, nada. They learned all that in the Gestapo. Quid. Glitz. Swank. Real slapstick... Sure, I can let them go. And the Consul with them... Get all these people out of here. Go, get out, hop to it! Clear out, fuck off! I'm kicking them in the ass! Watch them run for the exit, cowards! I just want to avenge our family, France. I know what I'm going to do, everyone will understand. See what kind of guts I have, sister. You're of the same caliber. Between the two of us, we'll make the war again and this time, we'll win. The truth is bursting. Yes, the truth will burst into bouquets. And no more recurrences... Even you, little sister, you'll be completely free. It will take one second, and then, poof, no one left. That's enough. The twentieth century wil be dead, and you will

*have understood. We've got to turn the page! This is all
pernicious. It ravages your insides. You're done in so fast.
They call it cancer. Claptrap, it's dust in your eyes. Some
infamous thing to put the masses to sleep. It's the Germans
who are irradiating us. You can make head nor tails of it.
We're cross-eyed, myopic, western moles. Historical beams.
Rays of past that pass over and over. We're turning into the
sifter of time, the funnel of the twentieth century. You've got
to let me be. You'll all be witnesses to the explosion of the
truth! You won't believe your eyes, or your ears. I'm going to
blow myself up and Germany will follow. In me, they
deposit their secret, their treasure. I am Nazi Germany, I'm
the horror of the three wars. They dared to shove it into me!
I'm going to destroy it! I'm going to blow their Germany to
smitherines, and for good! I'll simply hit where it hurts...
Flore, you're going to have to make a decision. You stay here
and we show them together, or you leave and you let me be.
You just watch the truth explode. And then, afterwards, you
do what you've go to do. But it will be over. We will have
won everything. You can make History with me, if you
want. I know you've had a bad time of it too, my Florette.
That the trains in your head whistled in the States. That
you were sixteen and your tinnitus prevented you from
sleeping or even resting. The Jerries, already the Jerries, but
we didn't know it! Already, the blue rays are having an
effect on you. I was happy that day, in Chicago, not to be
alone, to see that you, too, were suffering because of them.*

It's not generous, but still, it does one good to realize one
isn't crazy! I left shortly after. I did what I had to do! And at
last the night has come on which everything will end. It's
really going to end! And with such beauty... I'm going to
blow everything up! It's going to combust hard! The
Germanisery is going to leave us the fuck alone! The sky will
burst! Bring, brang, brong! A din... a big noise! And then
afterwards nothing else, no more German rumbling. No
more words in my head that come and go. I answer their
words in their own language. I tell you it dumbfounds
them, it gives them such a shock. They stop dead in their
tracks. "Luder," they say to me, but I don't give a shit. It's
their last word, their capitulation. "Luder," "Luder," and
then they disappear. I win the battle, and soon the whole
war. I found the solution and it will be final. It's got to
blow, fast, fast, may the blow strike. I'll cross the sky toward
victory. I'll be a comet. It will be historical. The German
tune can kiss my ass, I'll fuck it dry.

I feel really alone. He's singing, he's delirious. I don't
want to listen to him. My voice always rings false. The
women at my feet are like docile bitches. They're waiting
for a move to condemn me to death. To send me *ad*
patres or even *ad matres*. Violette may be waiting for me.
They make themselves small to better swallow me whole,
dismember me alive and shred me. I don't move. My big
brother's words are also my own. I'm spared them a little
bit because he nicked them all. He took on the anger,

the madness. I'm not crazy. I'm on the other side. I
could have been... I could have been just like him. But
I'm not and I have to leave this mental gum, the glue of
the past. Remove myself from it, and more than
anything unlearn it. Unstitch time, unravel the nursery
rhymes, silence the songs of war, the death rattle of
bombs exploding in my head every morning, the
reverberating sound of the German airplanes, the allied
bombers. And the trains especially. That incessant
sound, that discomfiting noise that I want so often to
tear from my skull. Even at night... Choo, choo, that
infernal rhythm of the locomotive that goes on and on.
Convoys, rails, cars, local trains, the railroad tracks, it
must all disappear from my vocabulary. I've got to put
an end to the vile war, the language of the past. Muzzle
German. Gag pre-war French and the French from just
after... The murmur has to stop, let me plug my ears and
let the words of today come at me head-on, slam me in
the sucker and bring me back to the here and even the
now. I only know life by what I've been told... And then
by everything that wasn't said. Silence transmits the
essential. Silence is talkative, it natters, it blatters. It
rings in my head like a car rushing toward a violent and
terrifying destination. I am not Florent! I am Flore
Forget and I must forget. Draw a line. Detach the hank
of the infernal spool, unstitch the trope of days, unfasten
the corset of History. That it may learn to breathe! I am

just Violette's daughter. And not her first son. I'm not worth much. Life can buy me... So, my dear brother, you've got to understand: I'm leaving you here in this German Consulate, I'm leaving you your destructive rage, your ungentle madness which, of course, is hurting me. But what can I do now? And even thirty years ago, or say even forty: I'm not petty, what could I have tried? I know it's my fault, my responsibility, that if I hadn't been born, maybe mother would have understood sooner that you weren't well. Who knows... I know that I must carry this eternal torment for not having been anything other than that Flore... But I'll live with it. It's my own destiny. I haven't got another one. Ferdinand has been calling you for a long time, a good long time. You resemble him when you're raving mad. You turn into Ferdinand. It's astounding. At least in the photographs, because we didn't know him, and that's the tragedy of it. He's asking you to avenge him. So maybe you need to go... I'm trying to convince you not to execute this plan that seems to come from far away, some war. But you're really furious, you hurl harsh words! You tell me I'm German and order me to leave. I'm embracing you, my brother, I'm coming close to you. You want to push me away, but you can't. You want to blow us both up, you and me, me and you. I know it... I'm not afraid of anything! I bid you my farewell... I'm taking you into my arms and I'm weeping and I'm praying. You push me far away. You want nothing to do with me! Your eyes are those of a madman. That's what you are. Or maybe just someone else. A man of another age. Born in 1889, one 12th of May. It was beautiful out. Does one recover from such a thing? And if one recovers, does he transmit the pain to an innocent grandson who quickly loses his mind? You are Ferdinand Hubert and I'm you granddaughter. I bid you farewell my brother, you whom I didn't like. I didn't even try. That's the way it is and I'm to blame. I was afraid of being swallowed by you, kooky Vesuvius, devourer of lives. You would have spat me up in one of your furies. I would have been projected from your maw of Tarasque. I was terrified of being the one who, like you, howled in the night, without really knowing why. Me, at night, I receive calls and I fly to the rescue of those in need, those who can be sewn up. I wanted to set myself apart from our resemblance to one another. Violette gemellipara, that's what I thought of her. Mother created two crazies, two monsters, two hybrids, two ignominies. From illicit couplings, she conceived two cruel carnivorous flowers. Flore and Florent. A bad start! We're *droseraceae,* Venus Flytraps, wild sundews. We devour one another, you and me, go figure, and now I've had enough... I'm sick of all these chimeric incests, these atrocious, imaginary copulations. I'm not Flora. In my own name, I castrate it, I tear out the flower. The flower of victory. I'm winning the battle in order to better renounce it. I'm not Antigone. You'll do your best. I'm leaving! Flore hasn't been born yet. For you, it's war. Your dismembered body, amputated of a fictional leg, do what you will with it. I'm leaving, Florent, and I leave you my bitches. These women with black veils who want a sacrifice, a cause, from history in order to take better pleasure in the past over which they rub their lecherous cunts, their miserable souls at not having been soldiers! That's exactly what it is! I'm no infantryman, no marine, no paratrooper. I wouldn't have wanted to have died in the Great War. I might have gone, but with a heavy heart... And I would have fallen in love with some beautiful German man. What can you do, I'm weak... But I'm not afraid of my shaved head on the public square. Flora would have denounced me at the end of the war. I am not France, I'm just myself. I'm the American, the one from the North, the snow girl. Here, flowers are rare, the seasons are brief. Me, I like cold countries in which war resonates without bruising the soil with its blows. Here, it isn't virginal, it isn't pure. On this earth, there were several ignoble wars that continue to be waged, but still, it's here that I can sometimes forget the past. At every intersection I don't have to read that a young man was gutlessly done in on the sidewalk. In the New World time is a bit different. Europe for me is decayed, withered. I forget in little pieces, in imperfect fragments. There are something like holes in me, expanses of yet uninhabited thought. I'm choosing my camp, that of a stupid life. A sprightly life. I'm not afraid of stupidity. And I need it. I'll have another serving at dessert and I'll be grateful. So, black bitches, women of great causes, sad, tragic furies, you who pester me, who knead my head, stop barking at me! All I can hear are your shrieks, your tinkling, your sordid little tee hee hees. Your airs of cirumstance and your exhortations to fierce hatred leave me like stone. Don't think your tittering touches me! Your doggerel is becoming hackneyed, I'm chasing you away, vassals. With the back of my hand, I'm sending you to the devil! That's where you come from. Go back there and die! May your pack run wild there... Your words are bullshit! Twaddle, what you speak! Your barricaded, shackled bodies posturing as women, I don't even want to see them go. Disappear, unruffled marathoners, inhumane creatures! You smell of pee, rancid, rotten. I'm too much like you not to hate you... I'm too much your sister not to wish you the worse! God knows I would have killed if I had been born elsewhere. But I'm from here and I'm holding on to this raft of Medusa. We sweat blood, it's true. Horror isn't far off. It's palpable. There's no shelter. One day, you never know... War explodes everywhere. Hatred can be transported. It's amazing how the lame world flirts blithely with its undoing. But today exists and I want to live... To take my Rose into my arms, lift her from the earth, get off with my cook, fall from cloud nine to flatten myself like a pancake in bed beside him. His neck smells like the chocolate he prepares during the day. Can one imagine such a delight? I'm tossing you aside, Erinyes, grousers, rabid ones. I leave you to my brother, to Germany, to horror! I leave you the typewriter of the past. I'm keeping the blank pages. Rose will draw on them. I'm leaving the basement of the Consulate without looking back. My brother could kill me. But I never happened. I'm not his sister. I'm nothing to him. He's ecmenesic. My birth is yet to come. The war isn't over. I'm returning to my time, the time to come. It brings my blood alive knowing that I exist. I stunned the dirty black wenches. There they are next to my mad brother, their mouths agape. The cops are rushing at me! We've got to split post-haste! My brother's blowing himself up and the consulate with him... There's nothing to do now. Just learn how to run. And it's blowing... Bong. Bong. Bring. Bring. Pshh. Pshh. Pshhh.... Disaster and liberation! It's exploding everywhere! I feel the heat rising along my thighs. I'm running. It's catching up with me! My ears are buzzing! I think my eardrums have burst! I hate that bastard, for having made me live through the war, now the bombings and the combat noises! That louse, he really will have made me sweat right to the end... Boom, boom... It continues. It doesn't stop! But I'm already far away.

I turn around, dizzy, completely stunned. All I see is a big fire, and the things of azure. Great torn sails trembling in the sky, darkening it for a time. Then it blows again! And there's nothing left! Prgg! Vroom... It's over. A pause suddenly like a terrible howl. It's just silence that has been tortured... My brother is dead, that's certain, and those women with him.

Now the sirens of life begin their song. Woooo! Wooooo! Here come the firefighters. I don't know where I am anymore, but the war has finally smashed me in the face. I had to live through it. Well, now. It's done. I even lost a brother. That's how it goes, what can you do... Mother, forgive me for not having saved him. I only thought of myself, like you that night when you decided that for you, it was over, that death was yours. I want to cry but the tears won't come. War is terrible, but you get used to it fast... Horror is familiar at the outset. An ogre that immediately chews up your heart. Intelligence fucks off. Everything is a question of survival. If something's still swarming, a feeling that hasn't yet died, quickly, we grab a gun, and kill it good. My brother blew himself up, and Germany, and the wars. This din pulling my ears apart should come as no surprise. There are the things that burst, that release all their wind. Constipated time has punctured its great paunch. It ejects, degests, exhales noisily. It's a stench, a real pestilence! Like

the saints, I hallucinate battle smells, the putrid ones
of gods and of the minced-meat of the Erinyes. The
century has defecated. A relief. My brother dies, it's not
fun, but it's my cure! The whistle of trains won't mean
anything anymore or will remind me that I'm going on a
journey, that the sea is open for me, that the beaches are
becoming tender. I take the train for the pleasure of it.
Apparently, that train exists. I take the train in training.
I'm a bit behind. At forty-five years, I must run better
than another. So here I am, I'm climbing in... There
are happy cars where the train goes choo choo and it's
not so bad. The TV wants me to talk, the cameras are
aimed at me. A declaration, a speech, words! What did
Létourneau want? I have nothing to declare. I'm waiting
for the armistice... They can embroider all they want on
my callow head, my bungled air, my body that trembles
without really knowing why. I just lived through the
war, for the last time. It's well and done. At any rate,
the second one. Soon, they'll all be done, there will be
no more witnesses. And those haunted by history will
blow their brains out. I'm impatient to be done with
those celebrations, those commemorations to their
heart's content. There are also the dead to come, that
aren't mentioned. The present yawns out of boredom.
It must learn that misfortune is there. All you have to
do is stretch out your arms. *Another war to forget that
one.* My great-uncle Raymond only said stupidities.

Really guileless things that aren't even funny. Howlers, blunders, he accumulated them. In single file, they came out of his mouth. War? I'll show you war! Don't you think that's enough? That we've had our assful of war? The journalists are assailing me. They're already on the case and must have called the hospital for my pedigree. I wonder what Madeleine will make of this affair. She'll find her way, for certain, in the next few days, to the front page, when they'll try to keep this thing wound up. The dust will have fallen, it will be necessary to bring the corpse back to life! I have nothing to say. I refuse everything. The police will interrogate me for hours on end. I'll have no story to tell. They'll quickly close the case. *He was a maniac... His mother just died... He went nuts... He was already nuts. Don't you think his sister, the surgeon, should have had him locked up?* The cobbler's children really do go barefoot. My brother, Violette's flesh, my dear brother whom I didn't love, how can I tell you at last that you are sacrificing yourself? That one day I would have been the one to have blown Flore up and then the planet to quell the noise? In families, there's always one who cops it, who's made to go through the mill, who goes to the front, to the front of the line for the whole family. He takes it right in the face. He has his head blown to bits for his whole tribe... You were the one. I was also the one. But now you've taken it all and I'm thanking you for it. Your death will help me to get through it a bit. Not unscathed, but broken, shattered, trembling with distress. Today, I am learning that I exist, I'm learning that the world exists and I'm saying: ... here I am!

Ten

TODAY IS BLOOMSDAY. It's June 16. And the world is
flowering again. And the world is shaking itself off. It's
blooming, boombooming, burgeoning, blossoming. It's
the day of dehiscence. The insects are buzzing. They're
playing at being airplanes and the flowers are bursting,
they're ripping open with pleasure. It's beautiful, the
air is orgasming, the air is groaning with pleasure
and letting out little cries. On the church square, the
children are playing hide-and-seek. Rose is wearing
a lilac dress with little white flowers, a dress Violette
bought before she was even born! *It will be for later.*
You'll see, time passes quickly, you'll barely have time to
turn around, and she'll be four years old... And twenty
years before you know it! This child is so beautiful! People
whisper as they walk past her. Nudge one another with
their elbows. Laugh, joyously. *Look at that little girl.*
What a doll. A real delight. It smells of birth, the future,
warmth, sweet, sweet milk. It's to die for! The church
is already full, friends, parents, many babbling faces,
speaking and immediately forgetting what about. It will
be a grand celebration. A beautiful ceremony. All anyone
can talk about are the flowers. Everywhere, on everyone's
lips. Extravagance, splendour, showiness. Mauve flowers,

violet ones, lilac, purple. Purple shades cover the steps, the great nave and the aisles. At the entrance to the church, there is a big sign on a tripod: "If life is just passing, on this passage at least sow flowers." The public greatly appreciates these words of Montaigne's. They would make it into their motto. They would stamp it onto their coat of arms. The public is blissed out. It goes without saying.

The guests climb the steps and stop a moment to read this little oracle. They giggle, embarrassed, cast timid, harmless glances at one another. They don't dare comment. Something holds them back... Best not to pay attention. A suspicious reserve. A sort of quarantine. Never in the fray, they prefer a tepid distance, the certainty of retreat... They won't change. Or perhaps yes, just for today...

It's Bloomsday, dammit, let the festivities begin... How the flowers jive! They look like dancers, teased little rats in tutus. The kids pick several of them and are told off. But they don't care. Reprimands are old hat. Childhood is made up of them. Of bravado, dares and plugged ears that refuse to listen to the brouhaha of grownups. So the children participate in the floral farandole, the ballet of heady, intoxicating smells.

There is waiting and waiting. Something is brewing. The ceremony will soon begin. But it's clear there's a delay... The priest is denounced, the organist criticized,

the celebrants castigated in quiet. The ambiance is that
of a feria. An unbridled chase of young bulls, some of
which are put to death, several summary executions
and perhaps also several mishaps or assassinations.
The day's breath is insistent... There's a little pile of
jism in the air, something good and sticky, viscous,
suggestive... Some lubricative mucous emanates from the
pleasure of a smutty sun on the skins of the company.
The bodies are happy, very over-excited. Hips sway,
they seem mocking, but impatient too for what won't
come to a close. Hands turn into fans. The wings of
the party. There is quiet beating, and then it quickens.
Hummingbirds, *trochilidae* vibrate the atmosphere. The
heat spreads. The ulcerated sexes swell, become blood-
engorged or moisten. Thighs are hot, rumps buttress
themselves, nervously parleying. The tapers in the
church run religiously. They illuminate nothing other
than the desire for abandon. The sun is so strong it
makes the stained glass glimmer. Even the garlands, the
crowns, bill and coo at one another. The hour is avid. A
big, fat, fleshy fruit. The guests wonder how to satiate
themselves. The girls mince, warm up. How sweet that
breeze would be on our breasts, on our vulva... How
good the rain's caresses... Points appear like flowers
seeking to pierce through. Men undo their ties, hanging
suggestively. People are downright sweating, it almost
smells like rutting. Children wail from time-to-time.

Some are slapped by their mothers. The boy's boys
take off their vests. Their plump bottoms swell in the
heat. Girl's girls kiss one another, cop a feel. No one's
paying attention. This is what is called a sacrilege. A
blasphemy, an insult! Let the sky ejaculate, let it relieve
us of the air, the madness of the hour, wiggling all by
itself, wagging its behind. We demand deliverance. Let
it begin at last! Grand organs, a procession! We'll sing
in unison, we'll strike up a *lied,* we'll even be able to
cry, secrete wholly. The anxiety is palpable. Some seek
out the toilets. Stomachs become knotted, fold in half,
empty and contract. The priest's house adjoining the
church accommodates those who can't wait, who are
twisting with need, about to explode. Their muscles
harden, stretch, impose a new rhythm. Base pleasure of
the belly, hoping for orgasms. The ceremony is a slut.
A right bitch. Gnawing at minds, spurring the organs.
The flowers become teases, they badger the bodices, flirt
with the wimples and low necklines, threading through
combs, hair, manes. They dress the gathered men and
women, get entangled with them, truss them, offend
them. Now they are all manacled. The assembly is in
chains. The shoes become small, the feet have stigmata,
their swellings burst inside the leather of shoes. People
sway to the rhythm. The heat is a tart and the sun,
a letch. The grass rustles, twists into phallic poses. A
dionysiac fete in full daylight, it's disconcerting! We'd

prefer the half-light, fresh little secrets. In the light,
desire rises in big gusts. Nature's orgy. A monstruous
coupling of the human with the vegetal. Today the
church is jacking off. Tossing frenetically. Its movements
become insistent and infamous. But the voluptuousness
doesn't give itself away. We wait, we wait. Pleasure is a
wave that doesn't rest. Young women, dressed in white,
distribute oranges and orange blossoms. Their breasts are
heavy, like the fruit retained by trees.

In the middle of this assembly, in a purple suit, a
cook becomes agitated. Here he is in the church square,
taking root. He grows, becomes enormous, his trunk
becomes giant. And then the summer ravishes him,
flowers open in him spontaneously. A poet hereabouts
would know how to decipher the signs of destiny. From
the day that offers itself, he could pick the languorous
afternoon, the substance of the future and leaf through
the daisy of time to teach us what will become of us
all. But here, *aoidos* are scarce. Like Hervé they don't
mingle with the delirious crowd. An endangered species,
they can only be found in greenhouses or old schools.
They're best forgotten... Alone is a cook in purple,
in aubergine. He is full of flowers bursting in him.
He sautés the signs, flambés them with porto, gently
prepares them, offers them up as dishes to the starving
hosts, in search of meaning. Will it soon begin? Enough
of this buffoonery! A heavy shiver in the distance. The

237

sound of music. Suddenly, the children turn serious. A ritual is being initiated. The kids know better than the grown ups which gestures to venture, the pageantry to deploy, the game and all the sumptuousness. A black car slowly advances. It looks quite sad in the yellow, laughing atmosphere. It's a stain on the day, a desire, a nevus. With it, a procession, a line of walkers smilingly following the obscene cariole. People carry flowers, they look like bouquets. The children are drunk with expectation, but they don't move and greet the procession bowing very low. The car stops just in front of the church. Angels jostle one another down the several steps. Their wings, flapping the air allow the gathering crowd to breathe a bit. Silence is a marvel. Who from this black automobile will emerge? A virginal bride with her coveted flower? A sainted slut who, in this blessed place, will be canonized today? Or better yet a pallid dead woman in her Sunday best? The cook knows. He moves without hesitation toward his beloved. His tail like a fat stem becomes a vine, curls on itself. A trellis and its unique, colossal clusters cover the whole assembly, proliferate, abound. The whole audience is there caught in the tangled interlacing vines of that good-looking boy. A strapping fellow, a sacred plant whose shaft is full of promise! Now the society is spinning, turning, knotting itself. It's entangled with this man's desire. Someone gets out of the car. It's

238

nothing but a tattoo, flowers, more flowers! A violet, a
rose, take form beneath a veil of exuberant petals... The
feet are bare, moving. Fragile as little bulbs. The bride
is a new species of flower. She is encirlced by feet of
furling rose gauze. Where did she grow? Out of what
manure? The angels reproduce themselves while she risks
the mute crowd, hitched to the breathless orgasm of
this handsome cook. One must imagine a carnivorous
flower, a creeping, climbing, arborescent plant that will
live as fodder. It's my wedding, so someone says. My first
communion. My baptism. My circumcision... It's my
funeral! Death becomes sexual. It teases me, chats me
up. I'm going to my obsequies. I'm marrying my cook.
He's waiting for me in the church square. Am I alive?
Deceased? Flowering? Wilted? Blossoming? Withered?
I'm but a flower, a perennial, not an annual. I flower,
I flower again and I don't know how. I'm cut, I start
up again, I come back at the charge with more vigour.
A floral octopus with spontaneous tentacles. Nature
is squalid, but it lives in me. Germination, eruption,
élan. I get out of the car. It's growing, propagating,
bursting in sprays. I'm suddenly in the presence of the
very place where the world explodes. The miracle will
happen, I feel it in my corolla, in my *rima vulvae*. The
vines penetrate me. They thread their way in my belly.
My transformation begins with my organs. They are
experiencing the fervor of my last time... My hair doesn't

239

stop either, undulating in curls, marrying in tresses. Several steps... I'm going to faint. The joy is so great. If I were attending my own marriage, it would also be a prefiguration of my floral funeral. But if this ceremony is my last one, the one in which I go into the earth, in which I'll plant myself for good, it resembles many great weddings. My cosmonautic nuptials with the great All.

I continue, the way is arduous. From the car to the nave, the steep path is treacherous. I follow the barefooted woman, the taconite Carmelite. I hammer the earth, I stomp on the brambles, the nettles, the thorns, the juices and sap welling in my vessels. Like a gravid helianthus, I turn toward the sun. Yellow and violent. Dancing in its light. Having reached the altar, slowly I kneel. I await the sacraments. The great benediction. The very anointment of my sap. My head gently leaning forward, I become transfigured: Timothy-grass, irradiant iris, epiphyte orchid, rose of Jericho, parmesan violet, *black sun, melancoly, blue watercress, wild gladioli, divine laurel, hyacinth, this myrtle bud gleaming, white lily, small bouquet of myrrh. Like a lily among thorns,* here I am. I am an oriental garden, a florilegium of days. I remember everything. Hours spent armed and disarmed, nights that wept, shivering with pain. Memory is festive. It flowers in the head. Its immortal aroma is the aroma of our impurities. I no longer commemorate. Even my flesh is prior. I grew

with the fertilizer of defunct history. Thanks to the fetid
liquid muck-water of memorable horror. It is in me
now like a joy sculpting the present. Time is not lost.
In me, it introduces itself, develops, reproduces itself.
My head is tilted, my modesty is intact. *Hosanna in the
highest.* A song rises: *Perfume pours out, it's your name.*
The ceremony begins. My love is diamond, emerald,
crystal. Here you are, my love, so elegant, so sweet. Here
you are my love, you who will pass some future through
me. I don't raise my head. I must capitulate. Allow
the twentieth century to live in my calyx. Here I make
myself into the bed in which the future lies, on which
the future sprawls. I am sick with love, in the fever of
times. But I don't raise an eyebrow. I am the daughter of
flowers, and thornless. One doesn't choose one's species.
One wears it as a jewel, a chaste talisman shimmering
in the foliage. I'm a pure and noble pansy, who carries
the light of the mortal vanquished within. I know
many dead. They flower in me too. They proliferate in
my body, make themselves into my progeny. They've
become flowers, often they wilt, but I watch them grow
back. I make bouquets out of them for myself. In death,
those tough geraniums plough the earth, those great
Calla lilies that vulgarly sway and rise audaciously on the
muddy mass graves.

My head is outstretched. Thus do I await my
verdict. I will say yes to everything, to my gracious love,

241

my daughter voracious for the life deployed in her, to the hours settled into my fertile breast. On the block, there are a thousand stemless, decapitated flowers. I extend my head. Flower among flowers. The assembly is mute. Moved. The livid seraphim. People are trembling a bit for me. It's my death. The priest no longer speaks. *Lord, my Lord, may your will be done.* And in the church, sick with the smell of souls, the voluptuous effluvium of these baroque bouquets, I suddenly understand that I'm going to lose my head. That my murder is imminent. The freshly blossomed Flower must die at dusk. At the dawn of its life, it must meet its end. Life ends one day. This is the one. I die today, June 16th. Forever. I say yes to something which is at last coming to an end. I don't have to wait anxiously for this to happen to me. I will deliver myself from the outcome by precipitating its advent. *Come, come, approach.* Death flies overhead, in the torrid nave where the overheated spirits will finally calm down. The sight of blood feeds the more sensitive souls. I was a surgeon. I lived off corpses, reddish hues, sanguinary desires, stitches, flesh to reinvent. Death always slipped through my fingers. I never understood it. I could never squeeze it in my arms, take it by the waist, savagely possess it. It was always fleeting, evasive. And stood me up! I'm done with that trollop who governed my life. Phew! I would never have known who death was. An old tyrannical bitch? A doddering despot?

Today, I'm ridding myself of her. She'll unveil herself, give herself to me. How I'll receive her... I'm dying on this Bloomsday. It's my ceremony. After, we'll close shop, pick up the chairs, pack our suitcases. The best things come to an end and the worse as well. I'm dying. My head is on the block. Drunken with lilies. With this beautiful protective cover of all-white lilies. The priest is very calm. The room is all expectation. Iphigenia will die, the winds will rise. And our proud ships will go to war. It will last a long time. But it must be done. It will be like a copulation, a big organic spasm. My cook will cut off my head. A giant scimitar has been confided to him. The actioning of the blade has been explained to him. He'll do it quickly and well. He knows how to cut flesh. I've watched him decapitate tough bulbs. Shlang! Shlang! Presto! He's a man gifted with not doing me harm. My head is sanctified on the wooden alter. My head is aureoled, it is becoming divine. Angels are wandering about, my gaze meets theirs. They are giving me kisses, love grimaces, quick winks of the eye, as devilishly, they lick the light flooding my face. Their chaste wings are thrilled at the idea of my blood. The assembly can't take it anymore. Women faint. They swoon with pleasure. The aficionados resist moving. Flore is going to die, and without a single regret. There she goes. And it's exalting. The baptism of life or of death. The goddess of a single day will find her burial place. The sun has good reason to have a hard-on. An unbelievable boner. Rose comes and deposits a chaste kiss on her mother's scented brow. I close my eyes. I relish the gesture. The common bluebell intoxicates me. And then, nothing at all. I hear them waiting. The angels and the mortals are holding very still. The cook approaches. His trunk casts a shadow. He approaches solemnly. He smiles upon me. Death. The blade will fall. I wish it happy. Shlang! Shlang! I will be no more. Dead... I am yours.

Now everything is white. It's snowing virgin stars. They fall gently and cover the world. Dust of a lost sky. Particles of the Immortal. As it falls, the occiput makes a flat, loud noise. The head pursues its fall, it rolls, making itself into a ball in the great nave. It doesn't retreat. It rolls on and on. Nothing other than a cabbage, a somewhat heavy calyx. Plock, plock, it resonates, rings strangely. The head on the tile isn't remotely discrete. It somersaults through the church. It's a tumble. Soon out of sight. There is hardly a care for the remains of celestial medusas who end too soon.

The apotheosis threads into the bright day. People won't have come for nothing. The crowd has dissipated. It speaks of the end. The body on the block quickly reasserts itself. And the missing head gives way to a new one. Flore is flowering. From her emasculated, neutered neck, several turions are soon born, and now here are

the sprouts. It starts to bloom. It grows more than ever.
The cook is proud. His beauty at last is being reborn.
Summer is at our door. It will grow from all sides. Life
will climb up our legs, it will smother us with joy. Flore
opens her eyes. Now I am sowing myself. There is no
assumption, not even an epiphany. I am made again,
I'm brown. The joke is on me... The farce is applauded.
A beautiful bawdy hoodwink. Definitely a trifle. I find
myself married indeed... To eternity. Thus is one born. It
doesn't end. Clever will be the one who is able to reach
the conclusion. The end is for films, for others, for the
defunct and the deceased, and even then... The end
doesn't end. One would have never to have been born...
Once it begins, it's a nasty trick. Everything grows back.
Even death. Here it is coming back. Die as I might, spit,
violate the universe. It continues to abound in the muck
of existence. Whether or not we cultivate life changes
nothing. Flowers always grow back. There's no escaping
it!

    I would like to smell good, embalm my absence.
My cook is there, I throw myself in his arms. He's the
new Europe, a Europe that doesn't even live over there,
that is simply a great chef and cooks up joy. His hair has
the strong smell of very good chocolate. I like memories
that only go back as far as yesterday, I like memories
consumed in little cream puffs. I like memories that
are quickly replaced by even better ones. I want more,

yum, yum, happiness, love. The new... America and engulfing oblivion. Let it continue, again and always. My God, make the crank of time turn infinitely... I beg of you, I beseech you on my knees. May the nefarious roundabout never stop...

CATHERINE MAVRIKAKIS teaches at l'Université de Montréal in the Department of French language literatures. Since 2000, she has published three essays, a play and five novels, including *Le ciel de Bay City* which garnered her several awards, including the Prix des Libraires and the Prix littéraire des Collégiens. It also earned her a short list for France's Prix Fémina. In 2011, she published *Les derniers jours de Smokey Nelson,* a *mise-en-scène* of capital punishment.

NATHANAËL (formerly Nathalie Stephens) is the author of several books written in English or French, and published in Québec, Canada and the United States. These include *Absence Where As (Claude Cahun and the Unopened Book), Je Nathanaël, Carnet de délibérations* and *We Press Ourselves Plainly.* Her translations include *A Cannibal* and *Melancholy Mourning* by Catherine Mavrikakis, *Poetic Intention* by Édouard Glissant, and the forthcoming *The Mausoleum of Lovers* by Hervé Guibert. She lives in Chicago and teaches at the School of the Art Institute.